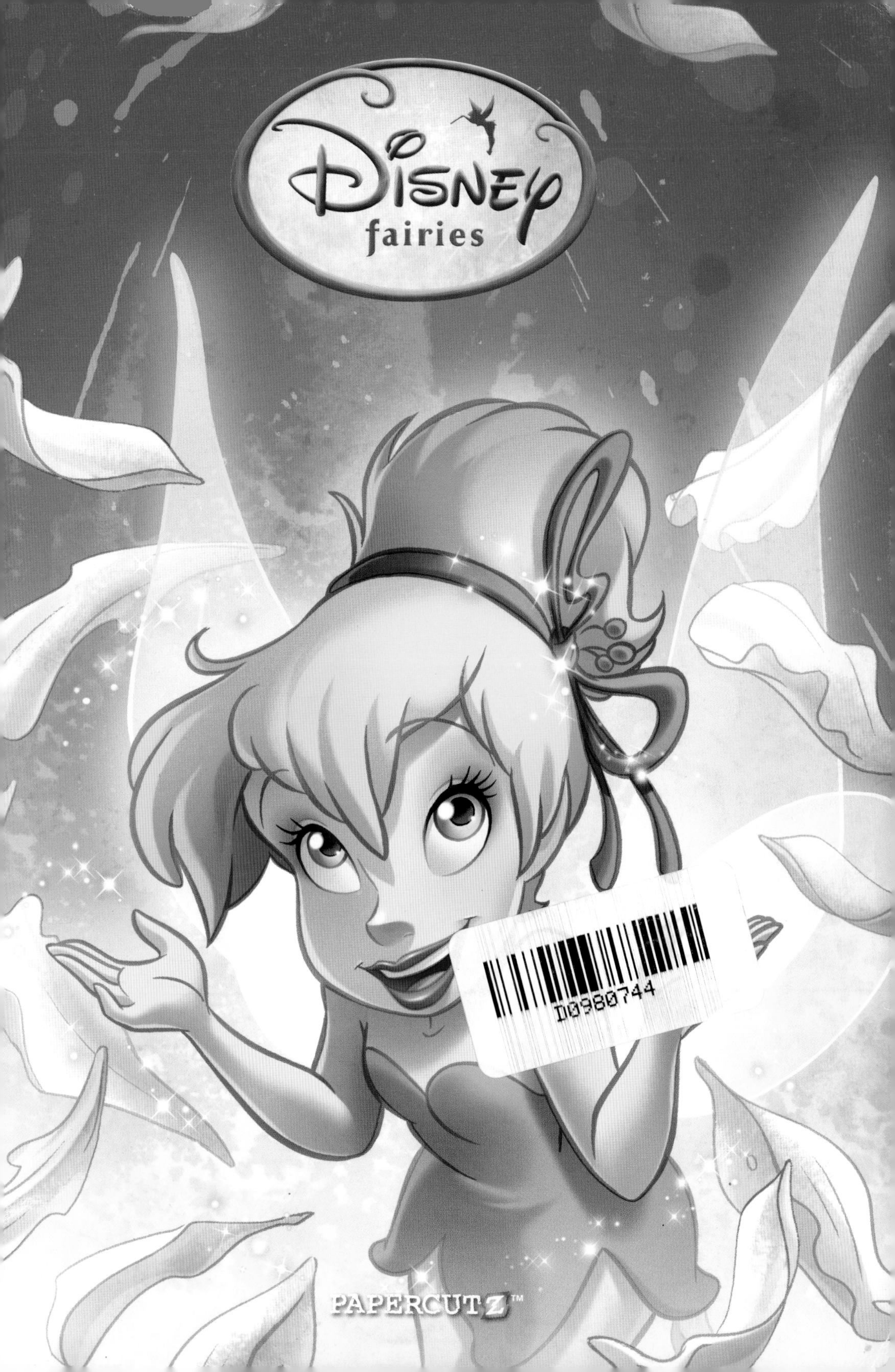
Disney
fairies
PAPERCUTZ™

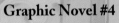

#6 "A Present for Tinker Bell"

Contents

PAPERCUTZ™

NEW YORK

"Too Much of a Good Thing"
Script: Paola Mulazzi
Revised Dialogue: Cortney Faye Powell
Pencils: Caterina Giorgetti
Inks: Marina Baggio
Color: Stefania Santi
Lettering: Janice Chiang
Page 5 art:
Pencils: Andrea Greppi
Inks: Roberta Zanotta
Color: Andrea Cagol

"The Scent of Snow"
Script: Paola Mulazzi
Revised Dialogue: Cortney Faye Powell
Pencils : Emilio Urbano & Manuela Razzi
Inks: Marina Baggio
Color: Stefania Santi
Lettering: Lea Hernandez
Page 31 Art:
Pencils: Emilio Urbano & Manuela Razzi
Inks: Marina Baggio
Color: Andrea Cagol

"Costy's Talent Quest"
Script: Augusto Macchetto
Revised Dialogue: Cortney Faye Powell
Pencils: Emilio Urbano & Manuela Razzi
Inks: Roberta Zanotta
Color: Stefania Santi
Lettering: Lea Hernandez
Page 18 Art:
Pencils: Gianluca Barone
Inks: Roberta Zanotta
Color: Andrea Cagol

"A Present for Tinker Bell"
Script: Silvia Gianatti
Revised Dialogue: Cortney Faye Powell
Pencils: Elisabetta Melaranci
Inks: Cristina Giorgilli
Color: Stefania Santi
Lettering: Lea Hernandez
Page 44 Art:
Pencils: Gianluca Barone
Inks: Marina Baggio
Color: Andrea Cagol

Chris Nelson and Caitlin Hinrichs – Production
Special Thanks – Jesse Post and Shiho Tilley
Michael Petranek – Associate Editor
Jim Salicrup – Editor-in-Chief

ISBN: 978-1-59707-256-4 paperback edition
ISBN: 978-1-59707-257-1 hardcover edition

Printed in China through Four Colour Print Group.
Printed June 2015 by Samfine Printing (Shenzhen) Co. Ltd
Samfine Industrial Park, Heng Hexing Industrial Zone,
Liaokeng New Villiage Shiyan Town,
Bao'an District Shenzhen, Guangdong
China

Distributed by Macmillan.

Second Printing

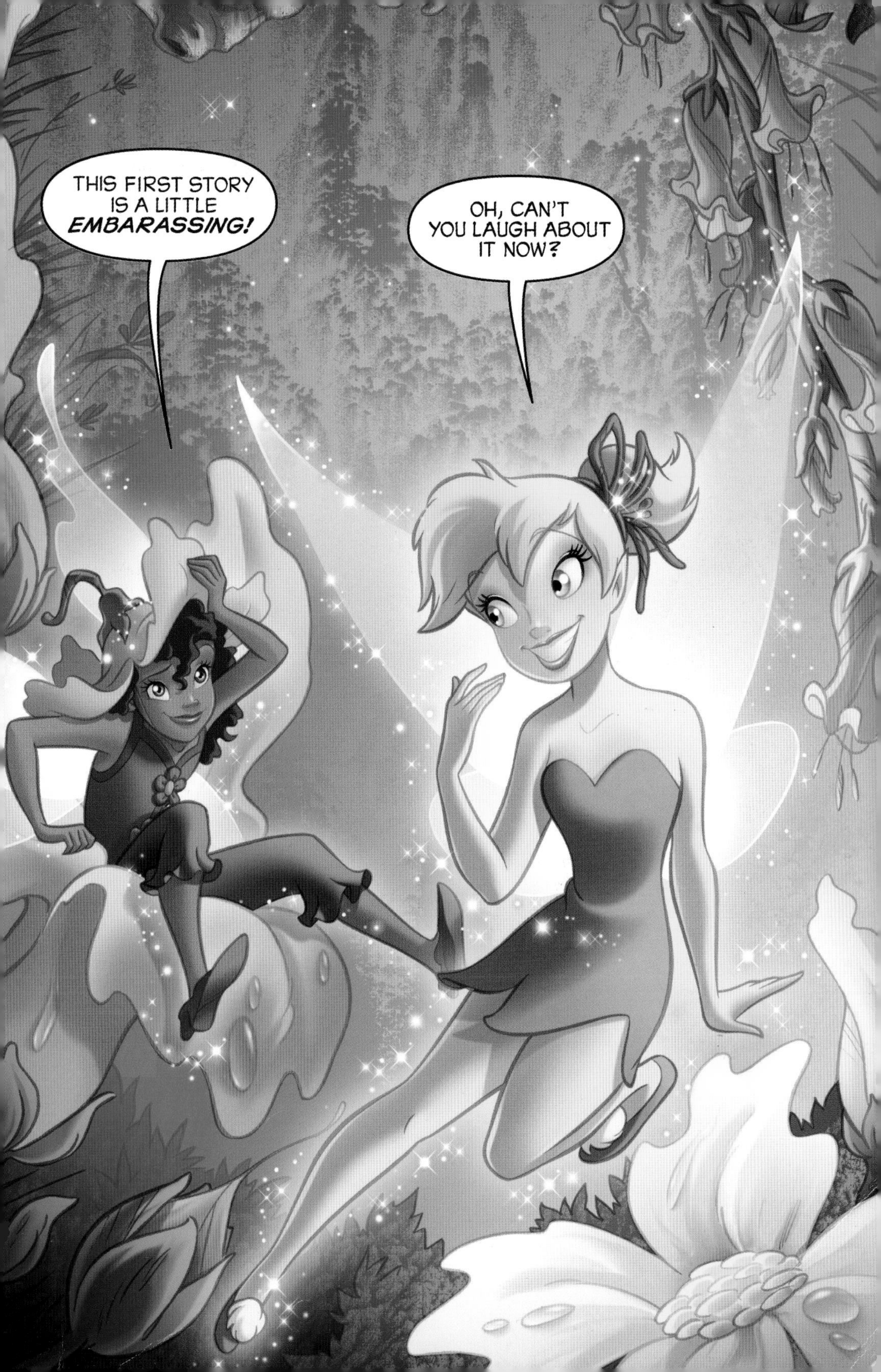
THIS FIRST STORY IS A LITTLE *EMBARASSING!*
OH, CAN'T YOU LAUGH ABOUT IT NOW?

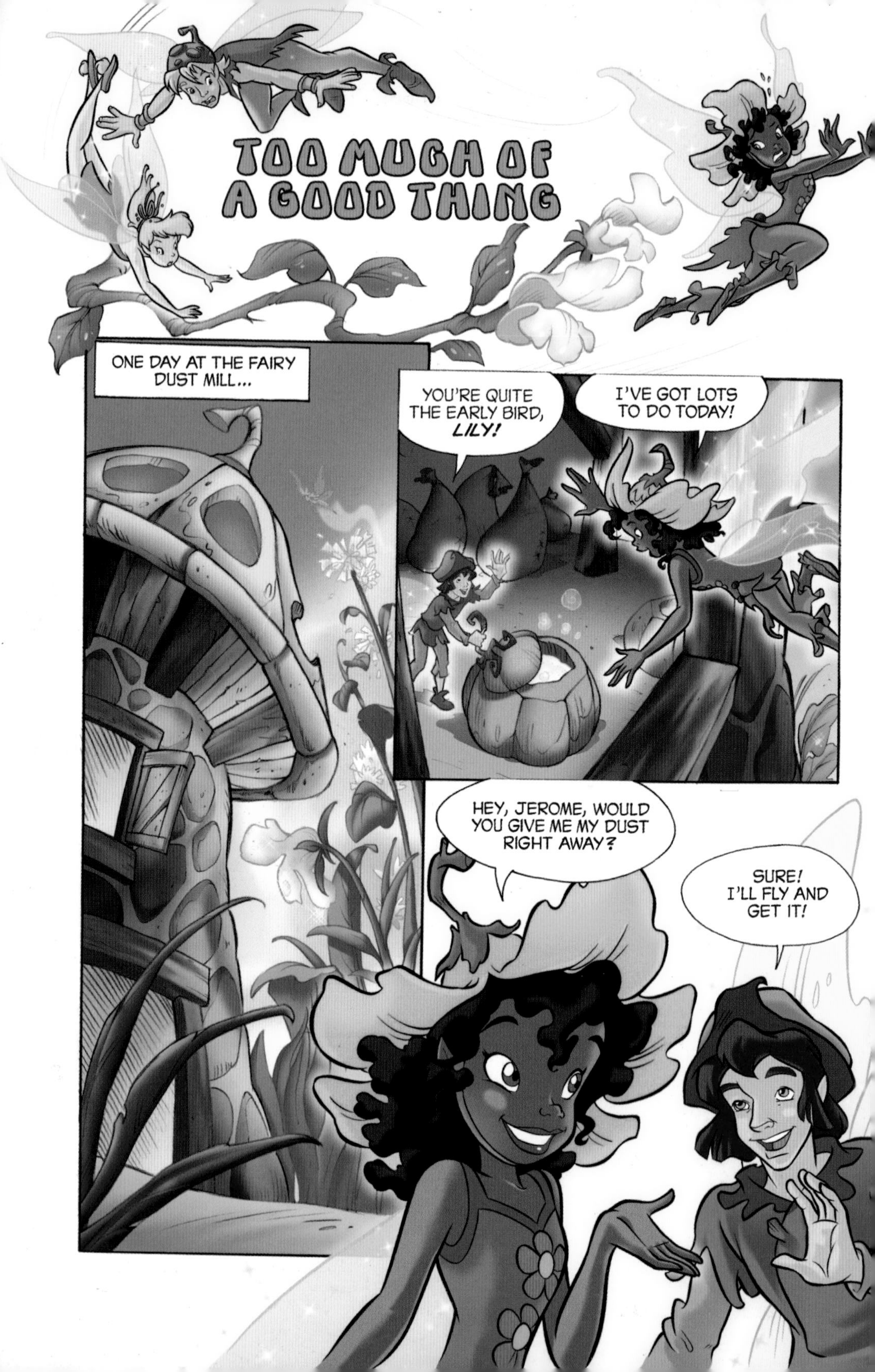
TOO MUCH OF A GOOD THING
ONE DAY AT THE FAIRY DUST MILL...
YOU'RE QUITE THE EARLY BIRD, LILY!
I'VE GOT LOTS TO DO TODAY!
HEY, JEROME, WOULD YOU GIVE ME MY DUST RIGHT AWAY?
SURE! I'LL FLY AND GET IT!

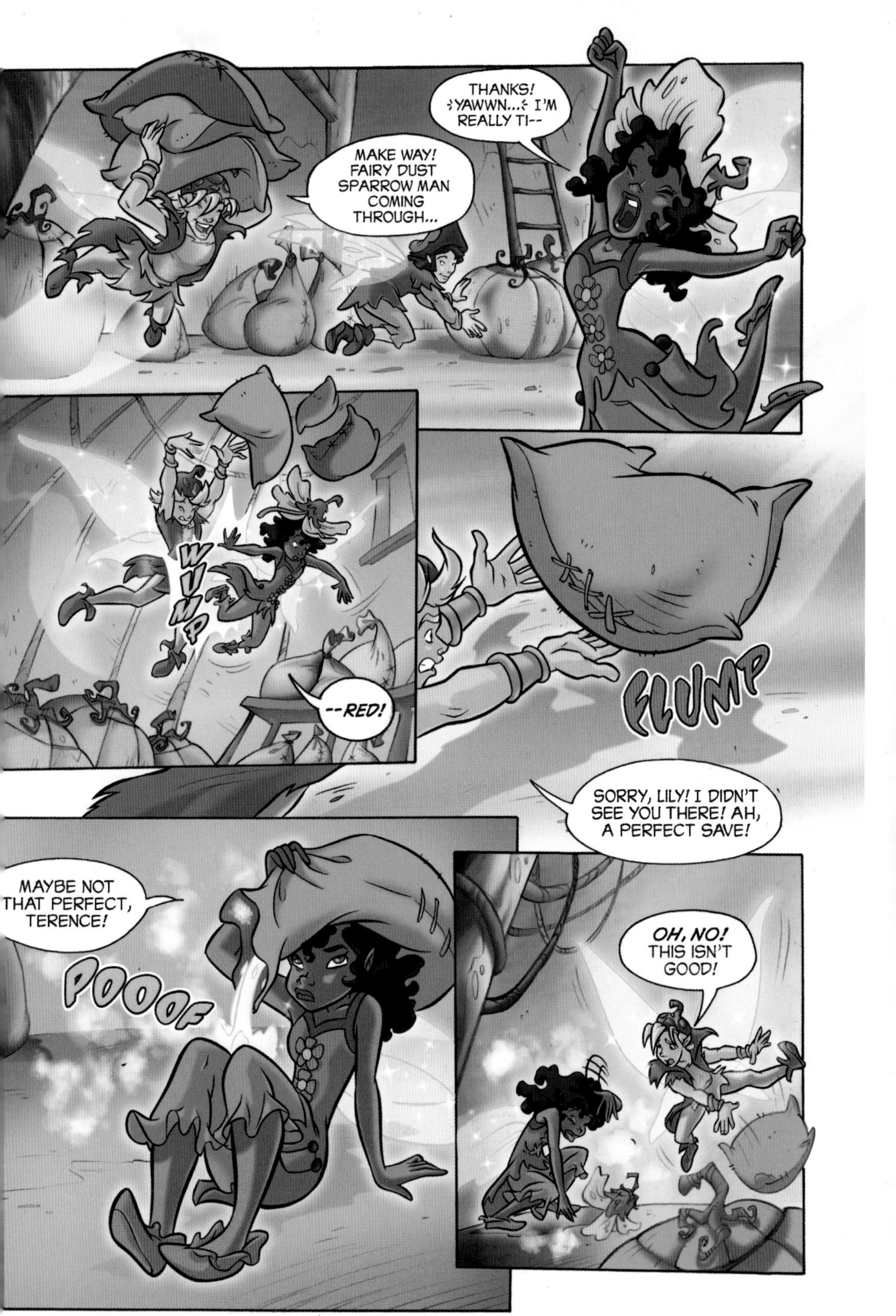
MAKE WAY! FAIRY DUST SPARROW MAN COMING THROUGH...
THANKS! ⊰YAWWN...⊱ I'M REALLY TI--
WUMP
--RED!
FLUMP
SORRY, LILY! I DIDN'T SEE YOU THERE! AH, A PERFECT SAVE!
MAYBE NOT THAT PERFECT, TERENCE!
POOOF
OH, NO! THIS ISN'T GOOD!

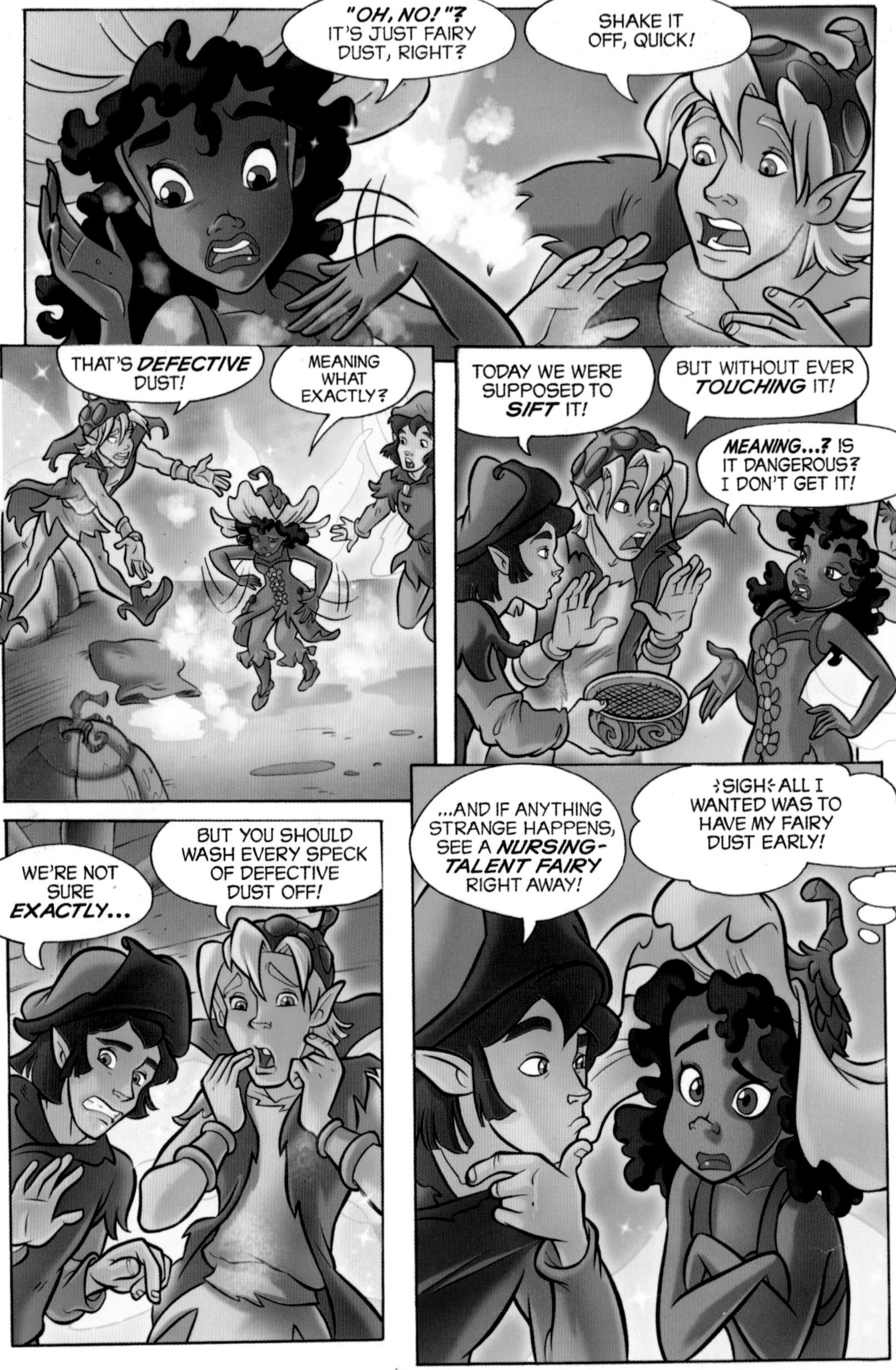
"OH, NO!"? IT'S JUST FAIRY DUST, RIGHT?
SHAKE IT OFF, QUICK!
THAT'S DEFECTIVE DUST!
MEANING WHAT EXACTLY?
TODAY WE WERE SUPPOSED TO SIFT IT!
BUT WITHOUT EVER TOUCHING IT!
MEANING...? IS IT DANGEROUS? I DON'T GET IT!
WE'RE NOT SURE EXACTLY...
BUT YOU SHOULD WASH EVERY SPECK OF DEFECTIVE DUST OFF!
...AND IF ANYTHING STRANGE HAPPENS, SEE A NURSING-TALENT FAIRY RIGHT AWAY!
SIGH ALL I WANTED WAS TO HAVE MY FAIRY DUST EARLY!

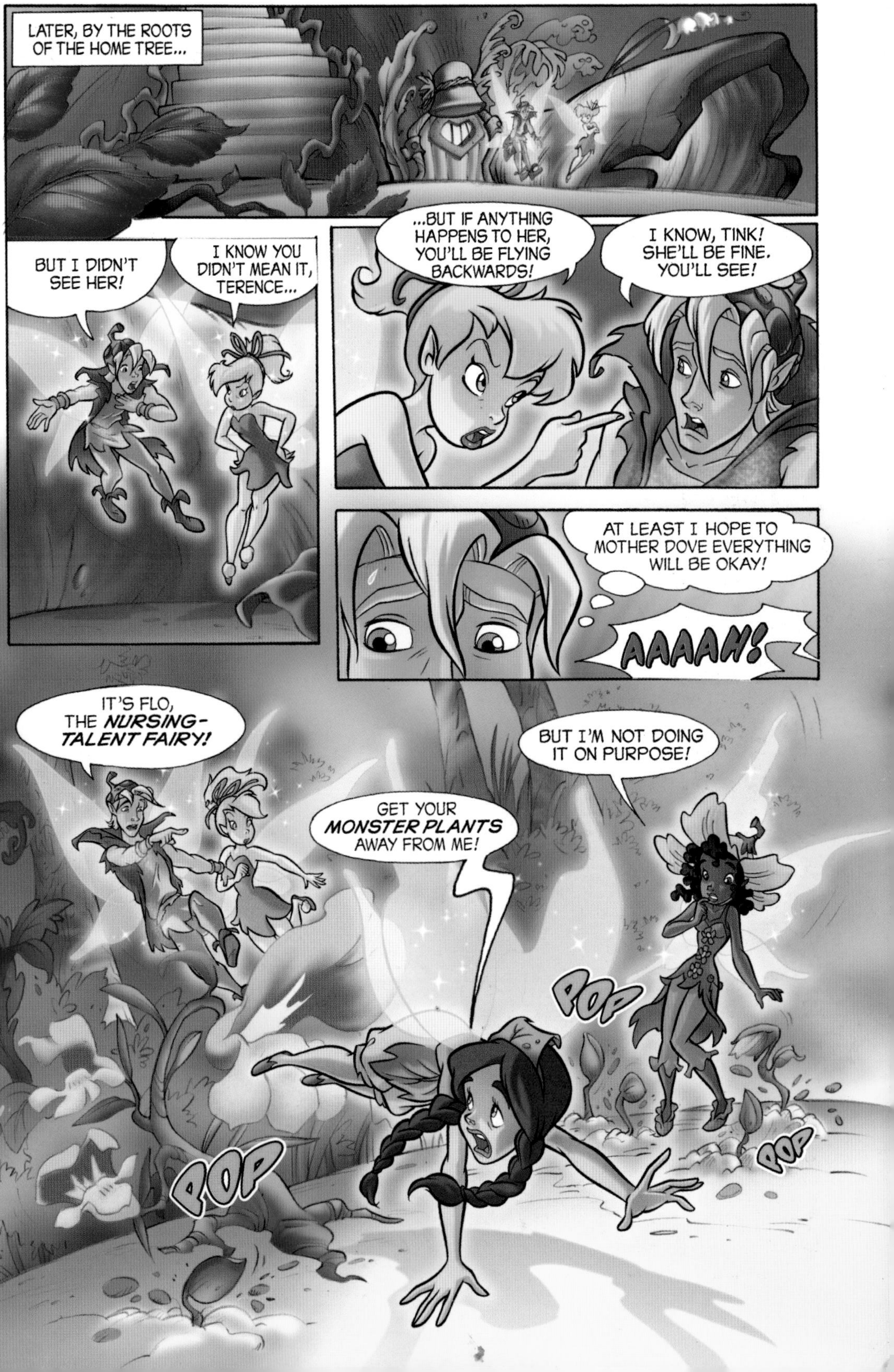
LATER, BY THE ROOTS OF THE HOME TREE...
BUT I DIDN'T SEE HER!
I KNOW YOU DIDN'T MEAN IT, TERENCE...
...BUT IF ANYTHING HAPPENS TO HER, YOU'LL BE FLYING BACKWARDS!
I KNOW, TINK! SHE'LL BE FINE. YOU'LL SEE!
AT LEAST I HOPE TO MOTHER DOVE EVERYTHING WILL BE OKAY!
AAAAH!
IT'S FLO, THE NURSING-TALENT FAIRY!
GET YOUR MONSTER PLANTS AWAY FROM ME!
BUT I'M NOT DOING IT ON PURPOSE!
POP
POP
POP

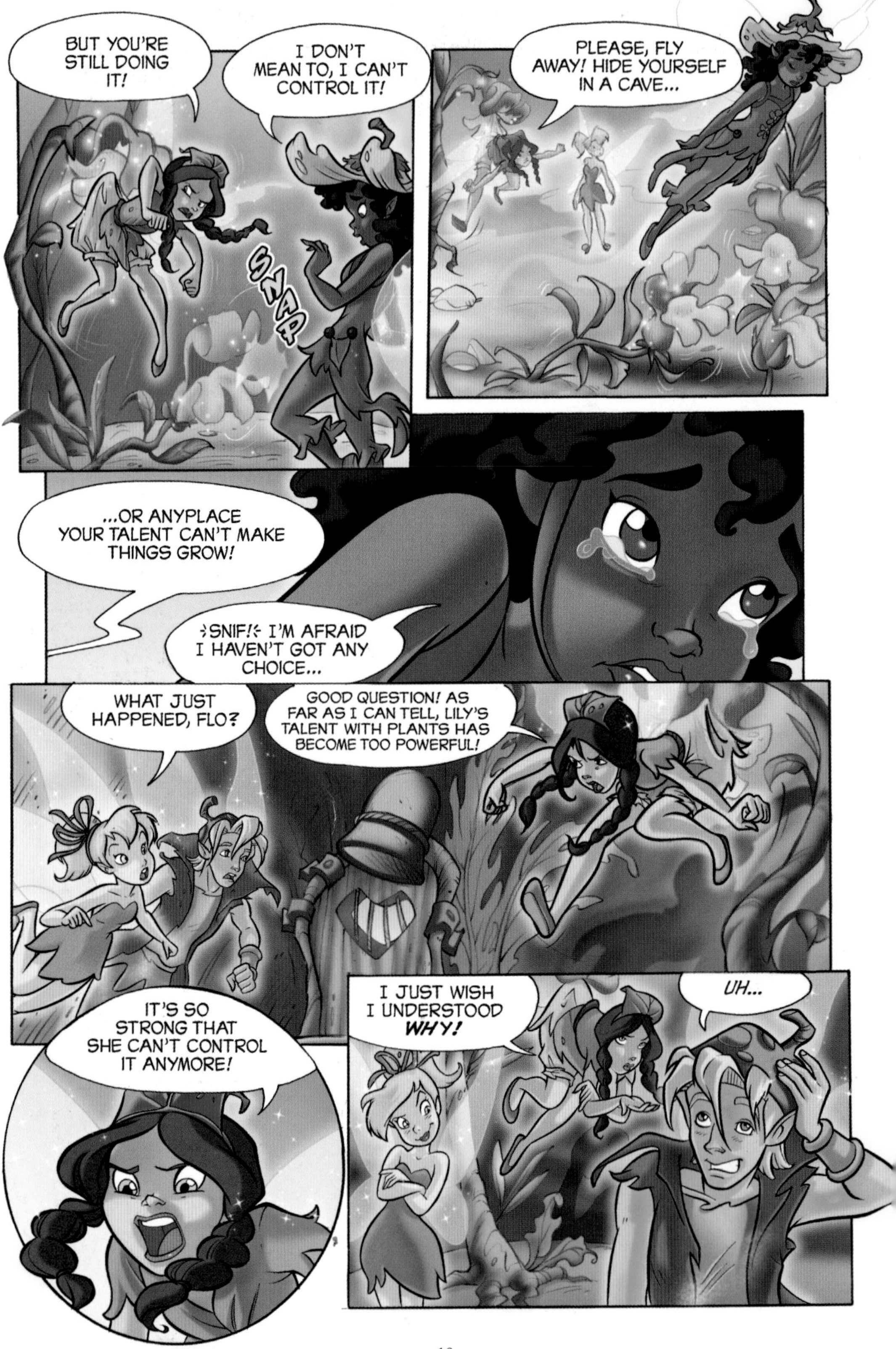
BUT YOU'RE STILL DOING IT!
I DON'T MEAN TO, I CAN'T CONTROL IT!
SNAP
PLEASE, FLY AWAY! HIDE YOURSELF IN A CAVE...
...OR ANYPLACE YOUR TALENT CAN'T MAKE THINGS GROW!
SNIF! I'M AFRAID I HAVEN'T GOT ANY CHOICE...
WHAT JUST HAPPENED, FLO?
GOOD QUESTION! AS FAR AS I CAN TELL, LILY'S TALENT WITH PLANTS HAS BECOME TOO POWERFUL!
IT'S SO STRONG THAT SHE CAN'T CONTROL IT ANYMORE!
I JUST WISH I UNDERSTOOD WHY!
UH...

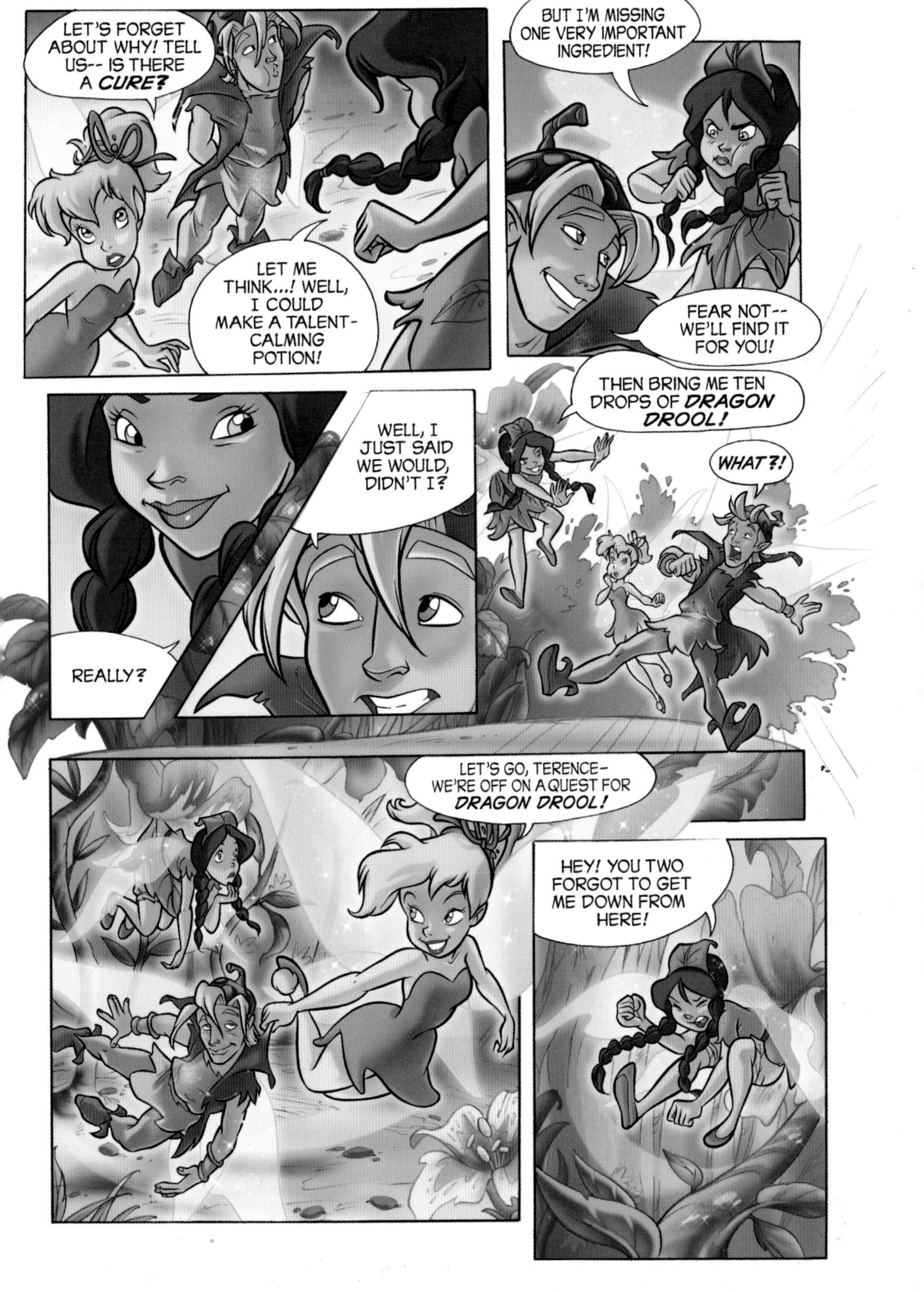
LET'S FORGET ABOUT WHY! TELL US-- IS THERE A *CURE?*
LET ME THINK...! WELL, I COULD MAKE A TALENT-CALMING POTION!
BUT I'M MISSING ONE VERY IMPORTANT INGREDIENT!
FEAR NOT-- WE'LL FIND IT FOR YOU!
REALLY?
WELL, I JUST SAID WE WOULD, DIDN'T I?
THEN BRING ME TEN DROPS OF *DRAGON DROOL!*
WHAT?!
LET'S GO, TERENCE-- WE'RE OFF ON A QUEST FOR *DRAGON DROOL!*
HEY! YOU TWO FORGOT TO GET ME DOWN FROM HERE!

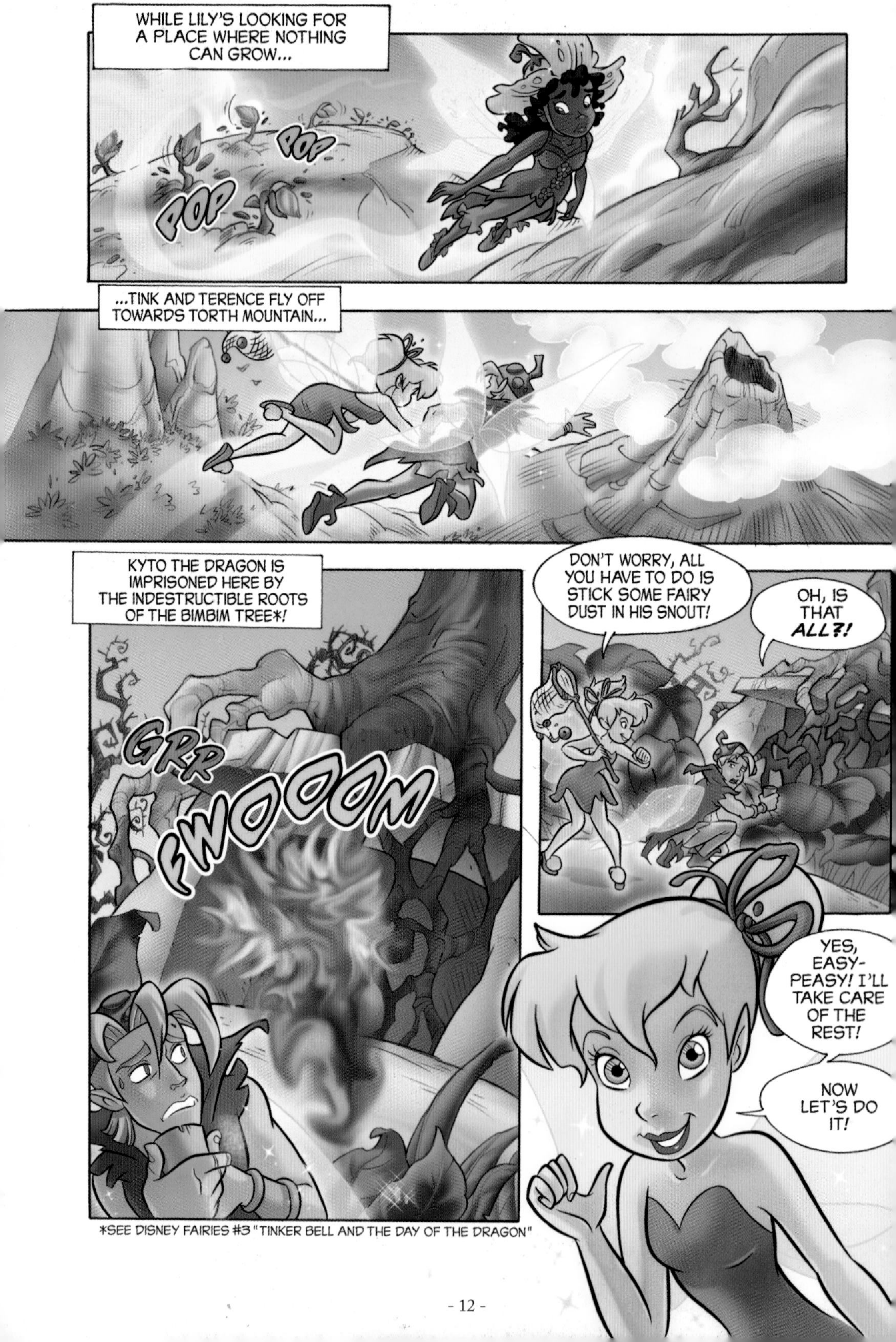

WHILE LILY'S LOOKING FOR A PLACE WHERE NOTHING CAN GROW...
POP
POP
...TINK AND TERENCE FLY OFF TOWARDS TORTH MOUNTAIN...
KYTO THE DRAGON IS IMPRISONED HERE BY THE INDESTRUCTIBLE ROOTS OF THE BIMBIM TREE*!
GRR
FWOOOM
DON'T WORRY, ALL YOU HAVE TO DO IS STICK SOME FAIRY DUST IN HIS SNOUT!
OH, IS THAT ***ALL?!***
YES, EASY-PEASY! I'LL TAKE CARE OF THE REST!
NOW LET'S DO IT!

*SEE DISNEY FAIRIES #3 "TINKER BELL AND THE DAY OF THE DRAGON"

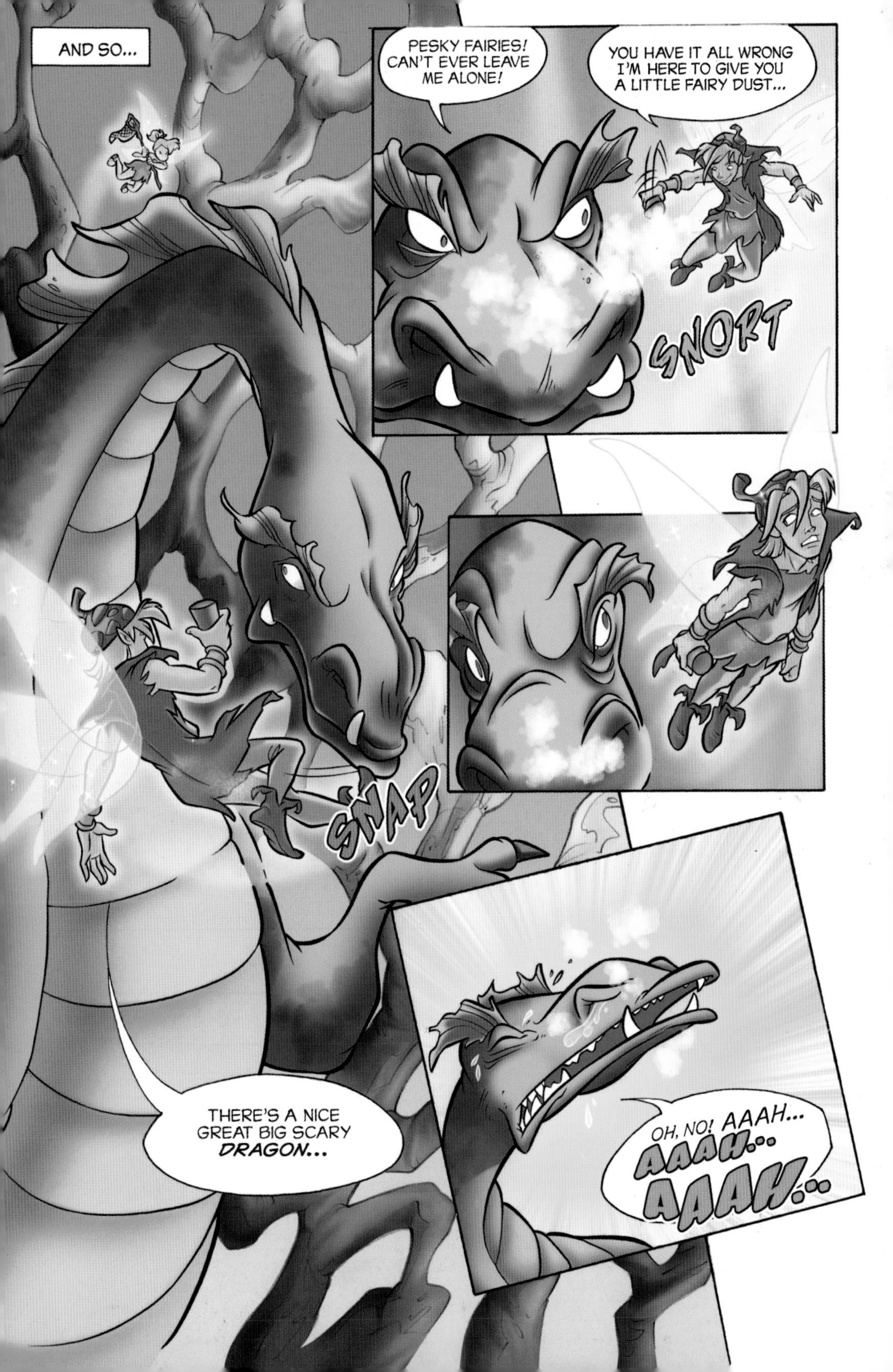

AND SO...
PESKY FAIRIES! CAN'T EVER LEAVE ME ALONE!
YOU HAVE IT ALL WRONG I'M HERE TO GIVE YOU A LITTLE FAIRY DUST...
SNORT
SNAP
THERE'S A NICE GREAT BIG SCARY DRAGON...
OH, NO! AAAH... AAAH... AAAH...

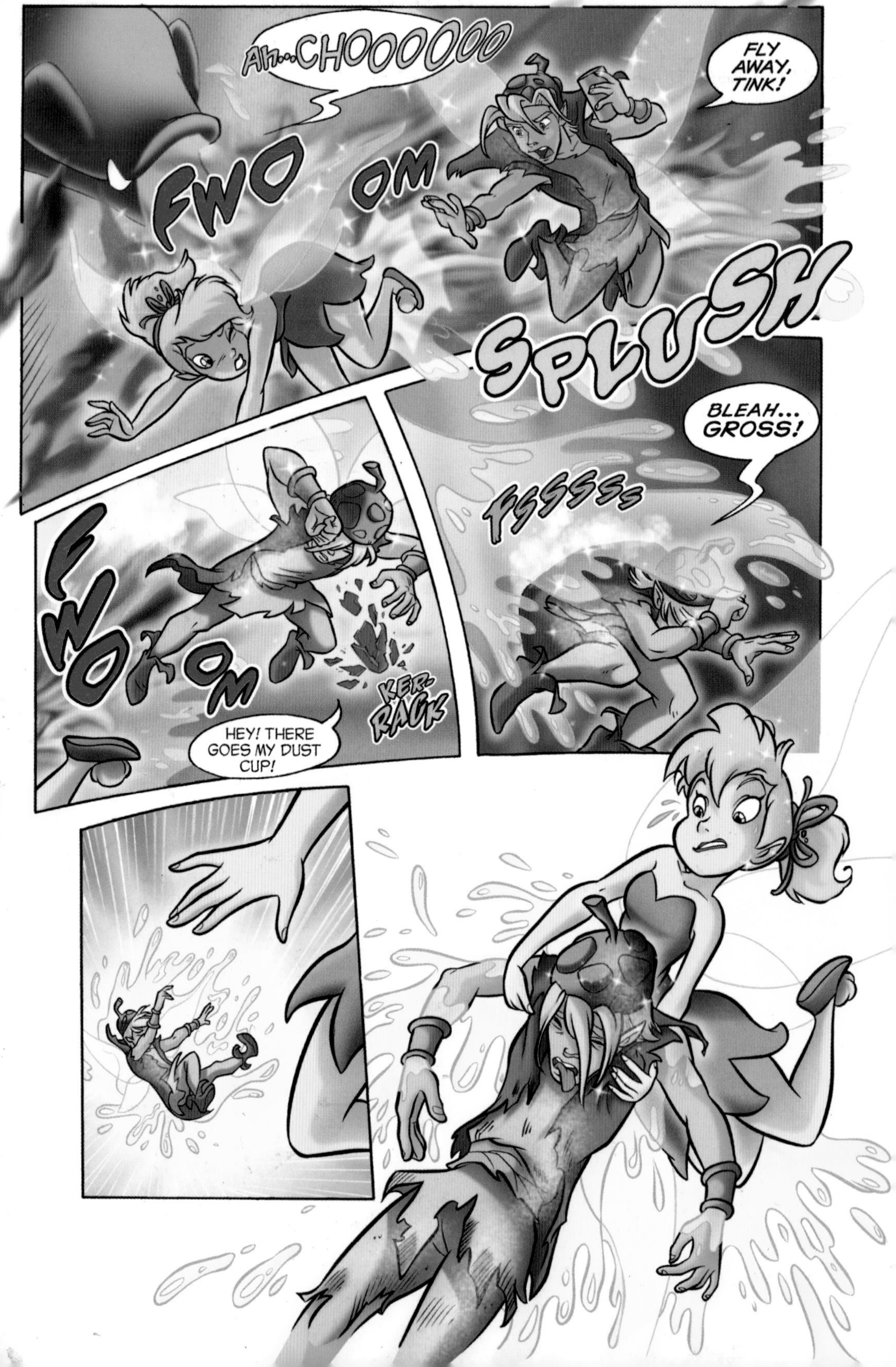
Ah...CHOOOOOOO
FLY AWAY, TINK!
FWOOM
SPLUSH
FWOOM
KER-RACK
HEY! THERE GOES MY DUST CUP!
FSSSSS
BLEAH... GROSS!

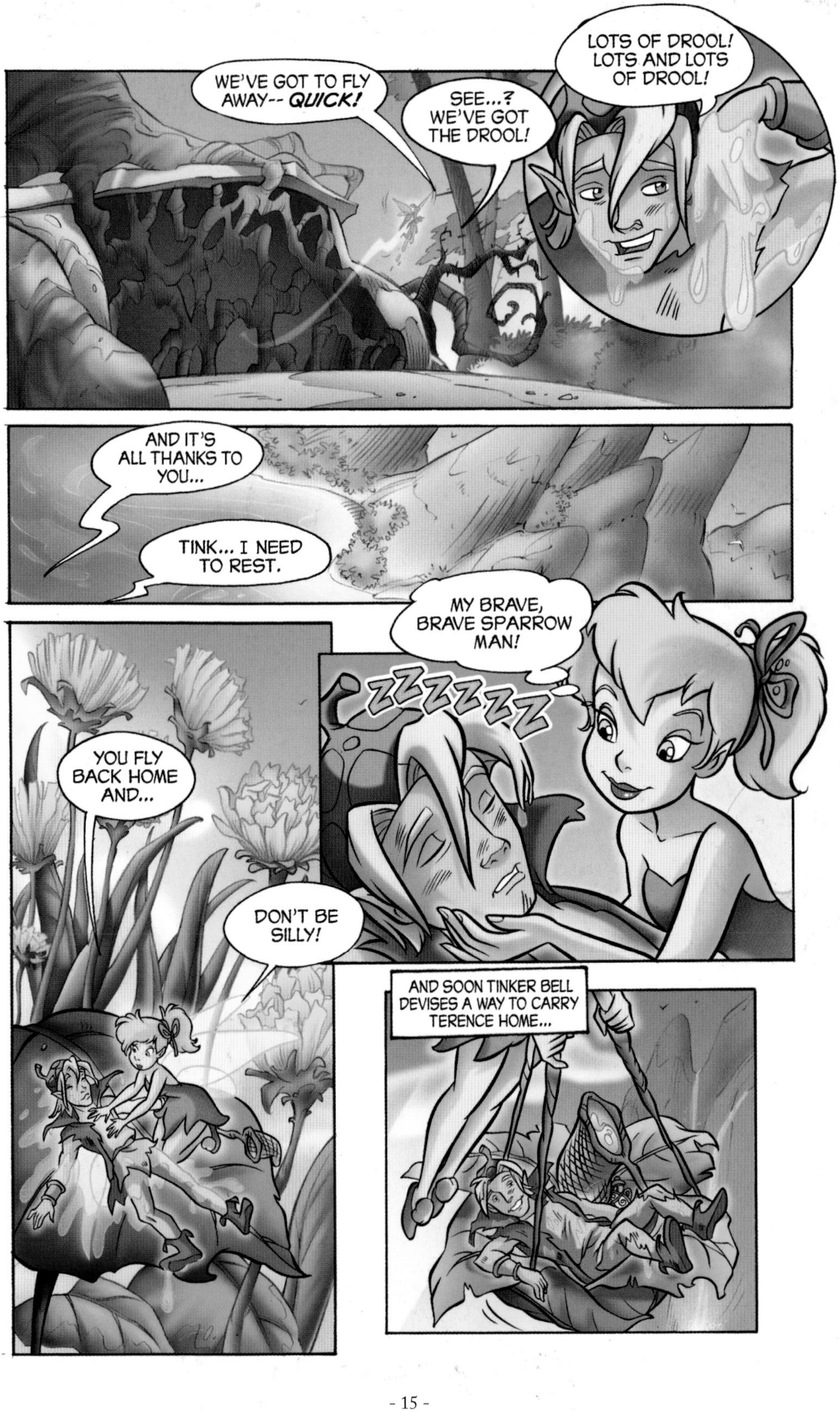
WE'VE GOT TO FLY AWAY-- QUICK!
SEE...? WE'VE GOT THE DROOL!
LOTS OF DROOL! LOTS AND LOTS OF DROOL!
AND IT'S ALL THANKS TO YOU...
TINK... I NEED TO REST.
YOU FLY BACK HOME AND...
DON'T BE SILLY!
MY BRAVE, BRAVE SPARROW MAN!
ZZZZZZZ
AND SOON TINKER BELL DEVISES A WAY TO CARRY TERENCE HOME...

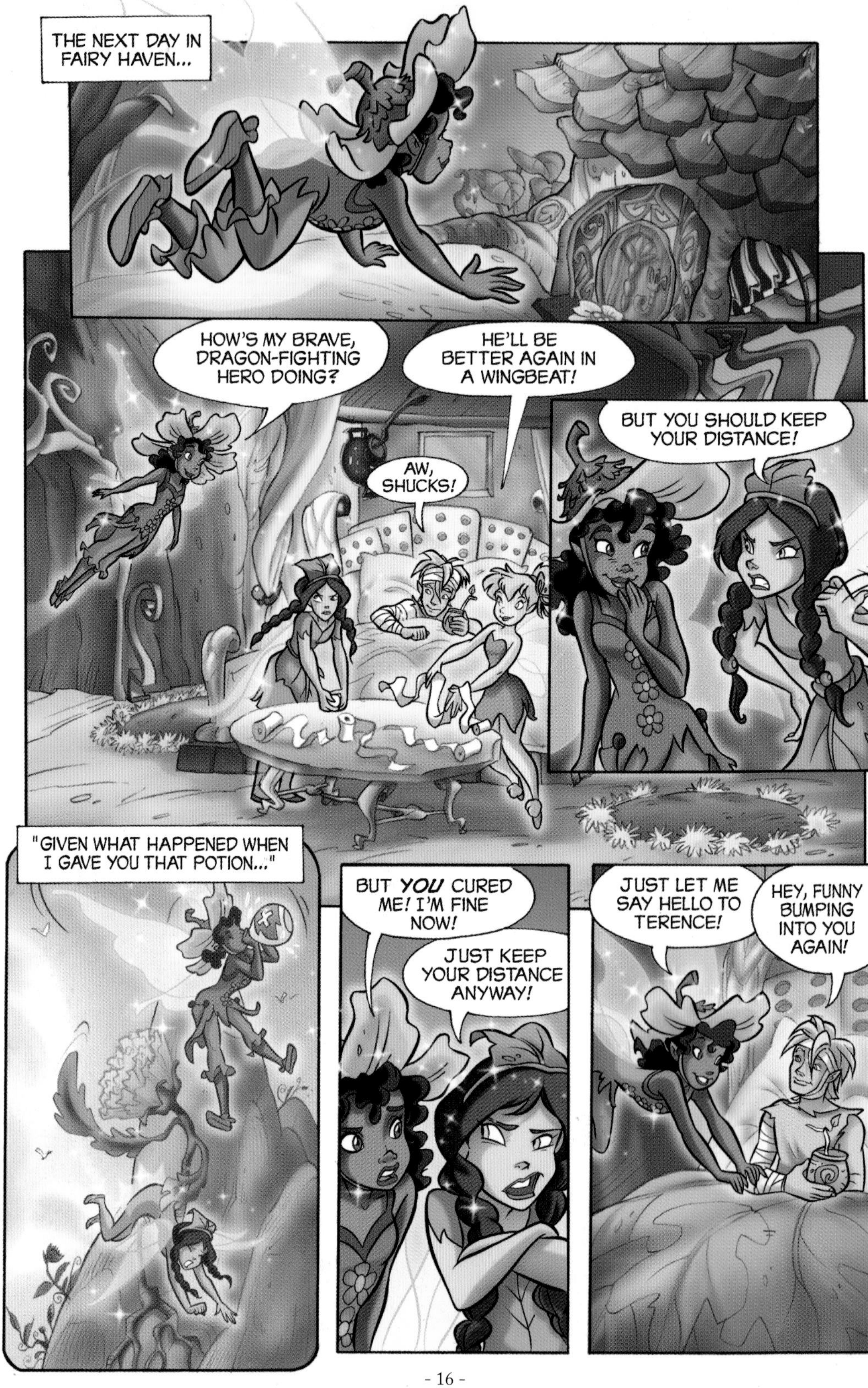
THE NEXT DAY IN FAIRY HAVEN...
HOW'S MY BRAVE, DRAGON-FIGHTING HERO DOING?
HE'LL BE BETTER AGAIN IN A WINGBEAT!
AW, SHUCKS!
BUT YOU SHOULD KEEP YOUR DISTANCE!
"GIVEN WHAT HAPPENED WHEN I GAVE YOU THAT POTION..."
BUT *YOU* CURED ME! I'M FINE NOW!
JUST KEEP YOUR DISTANCE ANYWAY!
JUST LET ME SAY HELLO TO TERENCE!
HEY, FUNNY BUMPING INTO YOU AGAIN!

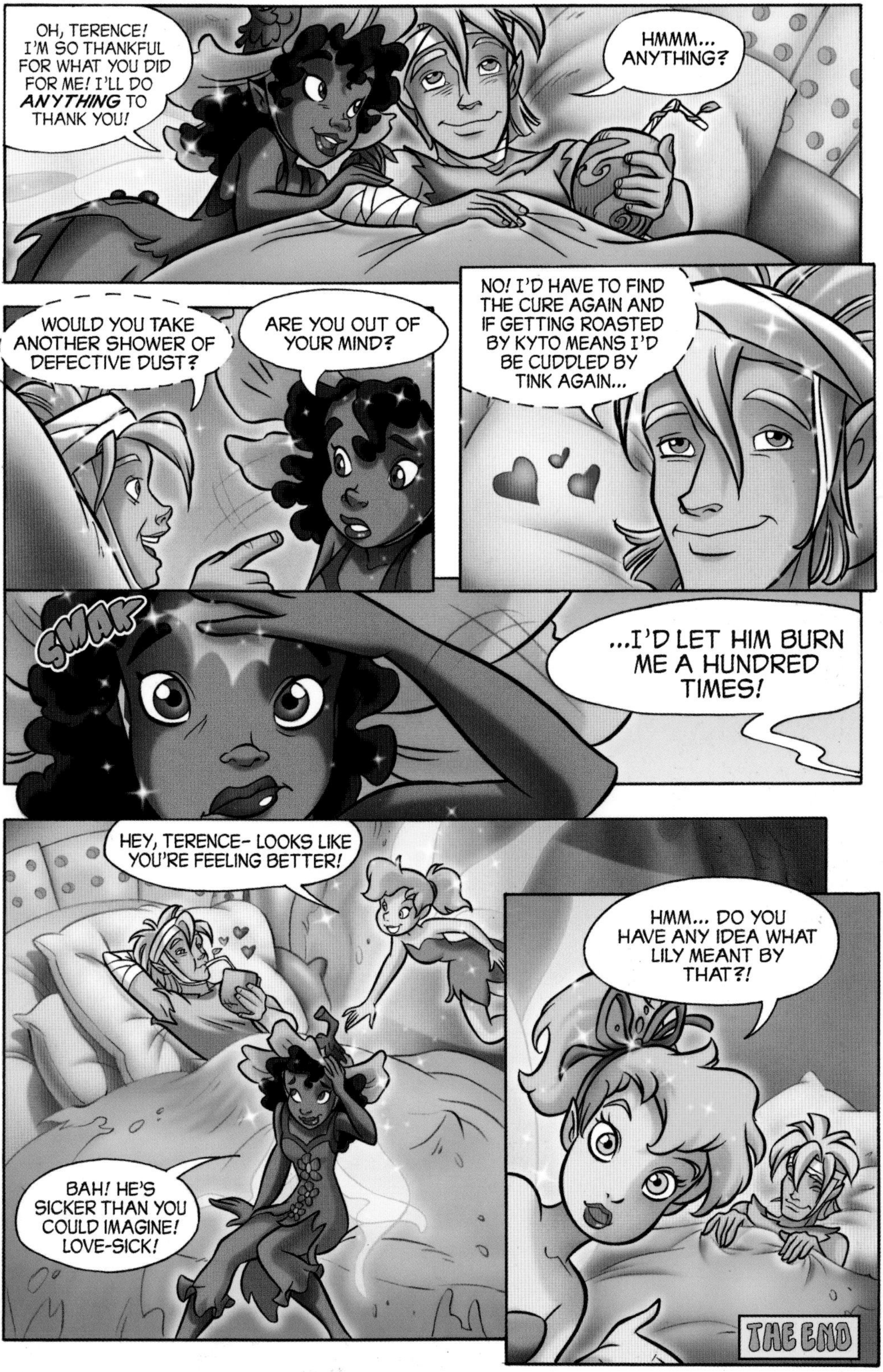
OH, TERENCE! I'M SO THANKFUL FOR WHAT YOU DID FOR ME! I'LL DO ANYTHING TO THANK YOU!
HMMM... ANYTHING?
WOULD YOU TAKE ANOTHER SHOWER OF DEFECTIVE DUST?
ARE YOU OUT OF YOUR MIND?
NO! I'D HAVE TO FIND THE CURE AGAIN AND IF GETTING ROASTED BY KYTO MEANS I'D BE CUDDLED BY TINK AGAIN...
SMAK
...I'D LET HIM BURN ME A HUNDRED TIMES!
HEY, TERENCE- LOOKS LIKE YOU'RE FEELING BETTER!
BAH! HE'S SICKER THAN YOU COULD IMAGINE! LOVE-SICK!
HMM... DO YOU HAVE ANY IDEA WHAT LILY MEANT BY THAT?!
THE END

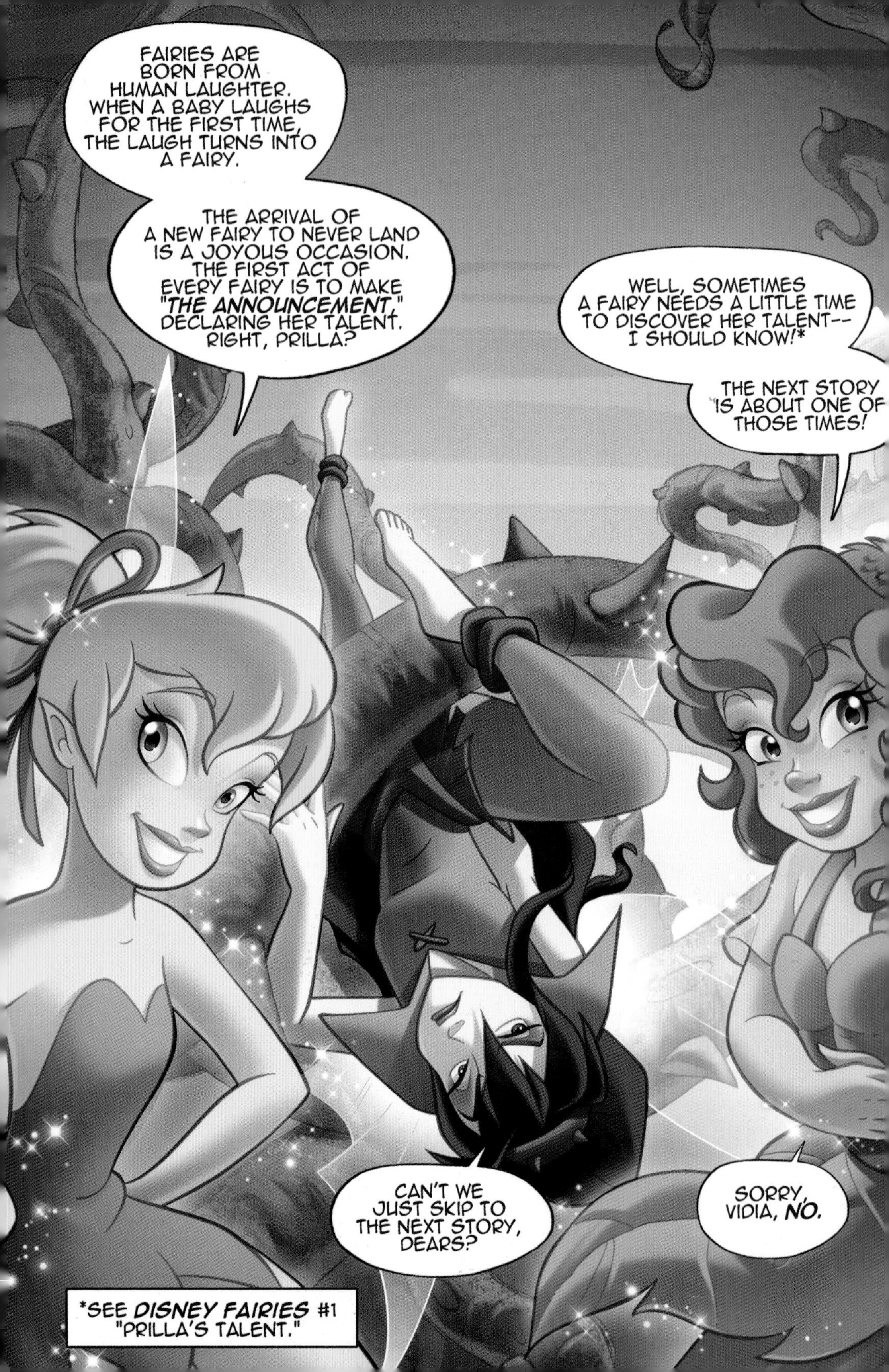
FAIRIES ARE BORN FROM HUMAN LAUGHTER. WHEN A BABY LAUGHS FOR THE FIRST TIME, THE LAUGH TURNS INTO A FAIRY.
THE ARRIVAL OF A NEW FAIRY TO NEVER LAND IS A JOYOUS OCCASION. THE FIRST ACT OF EVERY FAIRY IS TO MAKE "THE ANNOUNCEMENT," DECLARING HER TALENT. RIGHT, PRILLA?
WELL, SOMETIMES A FAIRY NEEDS A LITTLE TIME TO DISCOVER HER TALENT-- I SHOULD KNOW!*
THE NEXT STORY IS ABOUT ONE OF THOSE TIMES!
CAN'T WE JUST SKIP TO THE NEXT STORY, DEARS?
SORRY, VIDIA, NO.
*SEE DISNEY FAIRIES #1 "PRILLA'S TALENT."

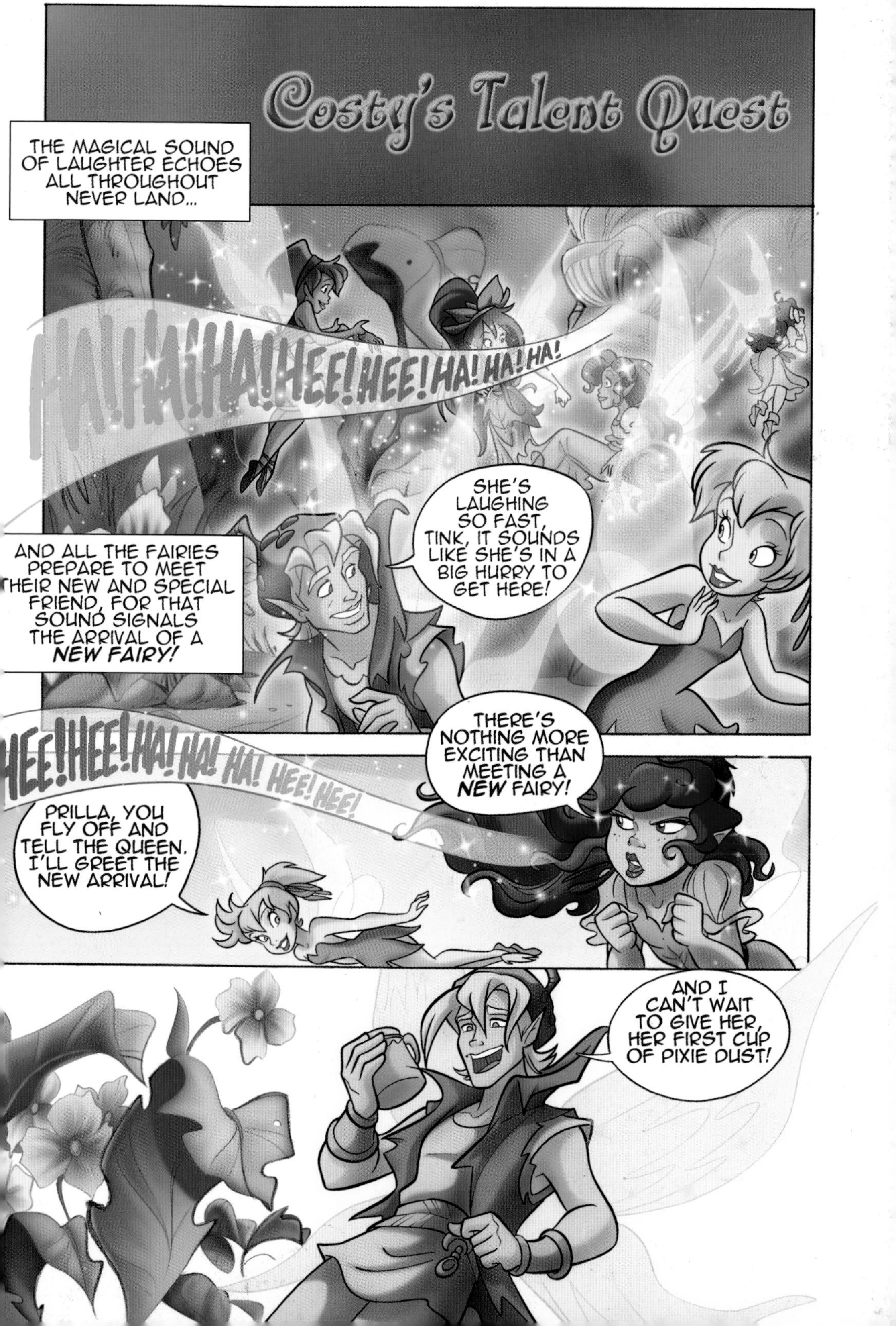
Costy's Talent Quest
THE MAGICAL SOUND OF LAUGHTER ECHOES ALL THROUGHOUT NEVER LAND...
HA! HA! HA! HEE! HEE! HA! HA! HA!
AND ALL THE FAIRIES PREPARE TO MEET THEIR NEW AND SPECIAL FRIEND, FOR THAT SOUND SIGNALS THE ARRIVAL OF A NEW FAIRY!
SHE'S LAUGHING SO FAST, TINK, IT SOUNDS LIKE SHE'S IN A BIG HURRY TO GET HERE!
HEE! HEE! HA! HA! HA! HEE! HEE!
THERE'S NOTHING MORE EXCITING THAN MEETING A NEW FAIRY!
PRILLA, YOU FLY OFF AND TELL THE QUEEN. I'LL GREET THE NEW ARRIVAL!
AND I CAN'T WAIT TO GIVE HER, HER FIRST CUP OF PIXIE DUST!

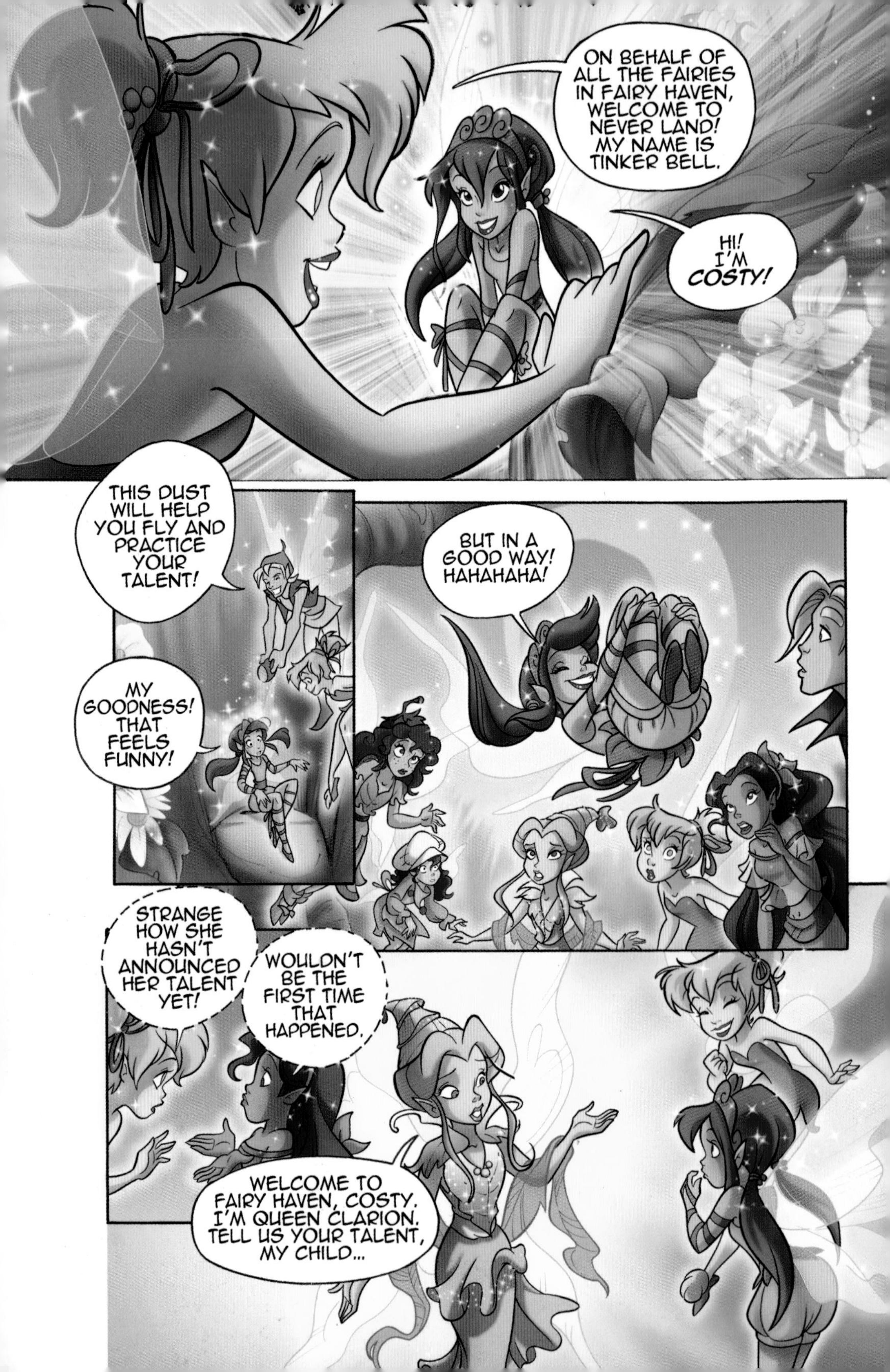
ON BEHALF OF ALL THE FAIRIES IN FAIRY HAVEN, WELCOME TO NEVER LAND! MY NAME IS TINKER BELL.
HI! I'M COSTY!
THIS DUST WILL HELP YOU FLY AND PRACTICE YOUR TALENT!
MY GOODNESS! THAT FEELS FUNNY!
BUT IN A GOOD WAY! HAHAHAHA!
STRANGE HOW SHE HASN'T ANNOUNCED HER TALENT YET!
WOULDN'T BE THE FIRST TIME THAT HAPPENED.
WELCOME TO FAIRY HAVEN, COSTY. I'M QUEEN CLARION. TELL US YOUR TALENT, MY CHILD...

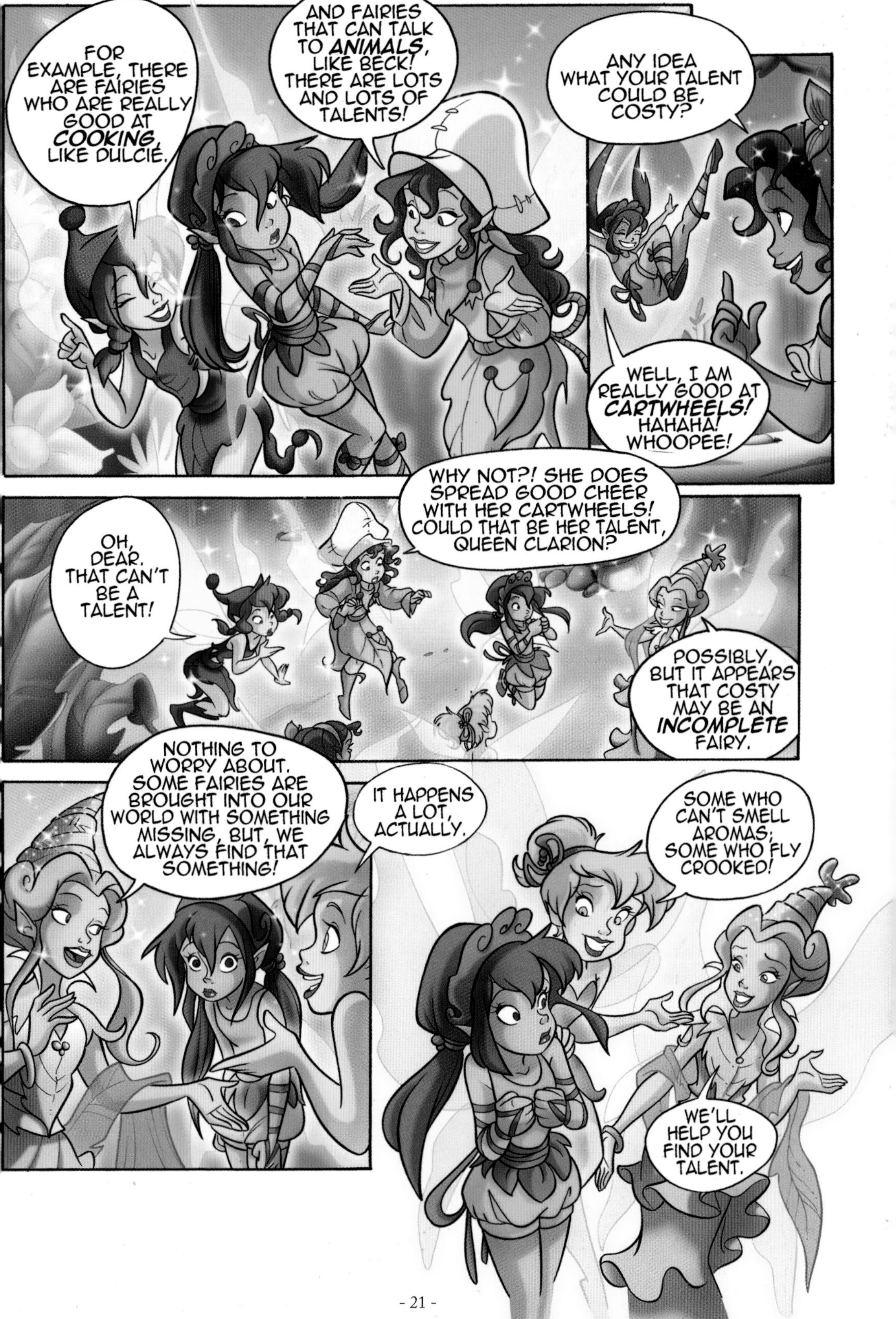
FOR EXAMPLE, THERE ARE FAIRIES WHO ARE REALLY GOOD AT COOKING, LIKE DULCIE.
AND FAIRIES THAT CAN TALK TO ANIMALS, LIKE BECK! THERE ARE LOTS AND LOTS OF TALENTS!
ANY IDEA WHAT YOUR TALENT COULD BE, COSTY?
WELL, I AM REALLY GOOD AT CARTWHEELS! HAHAHA! WHOOPEE!
OH, DEAR. THAT CAN'T BE A TALENT!
WHY NOT?! SHE DOES SPREAD GOOD CHEER WITH HER CARTWHEELS! COULD THAT BE HER TALENT, QUEEN CLARION?
POSSIBLY, BUT IT APPEARS THAT COSTY MAY BE AN INCOMPLETE FAIRY.
NOTHING TO WORRY ABOUT. SOME FAIRIES ARE BROUGHT INTO OUR WORLD WITH SOMETHING MISSING, BUT, WE ALWAYS FIND THAT SOMETHING!
IT HAPPENS A LOT, ACTUALLY.
SOME WHO CAN'T SMELL AROMAS; SOME WHO FLY CROOKED!
WE'LL HELP YOU FIND YOUR TALENT.

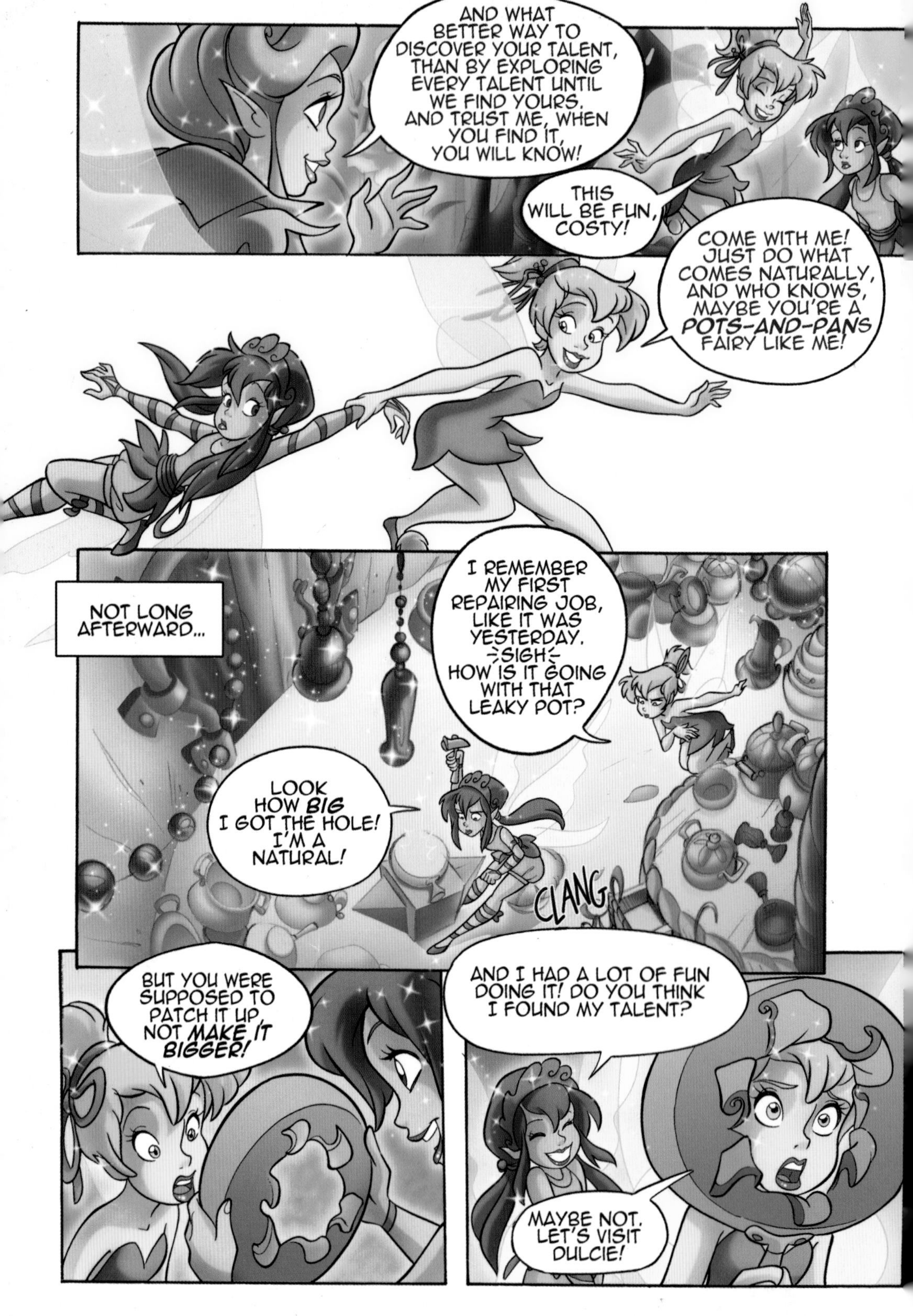
AND WHAT BETTER WAY TO DISCOVER YOUR TALENT, THAN BY EXPLORING EVERY TALENT UNTIL WE FIND YOURS. AND TRUST ME, WHEN YOU FIND IT, YOU WILL KNOW!
THIS WILL BE FUN, COSTY!
COME WITH ME! JUST DO WHAT COMES NATURALLY, AND WHO KNOWS, MAYBE YOU'RE A POTS-AND-PANS FAIRY LIKE ME!
NOT LONG AFTERWARD...
I REMEMBER MY FIRST REPAIRING JOB, LIKE IT WAS YESTERDAY. SIGH HOW IS IT GOING WITH THAT LEAKY POT?
LOOK HOW BIG I GOT THE HOLE! I'M A NATURAL!
CLANG
BUT YOU WERE SUPPOSED TO PATCH IT UP, NOT MAKE IT BIGGER!
AND I HAD A LOT OF FUN DOING IT! DO YOU THINK I FOUND MY TALENT?
MAYBE NOT. LET'S VISIT DULCIE!

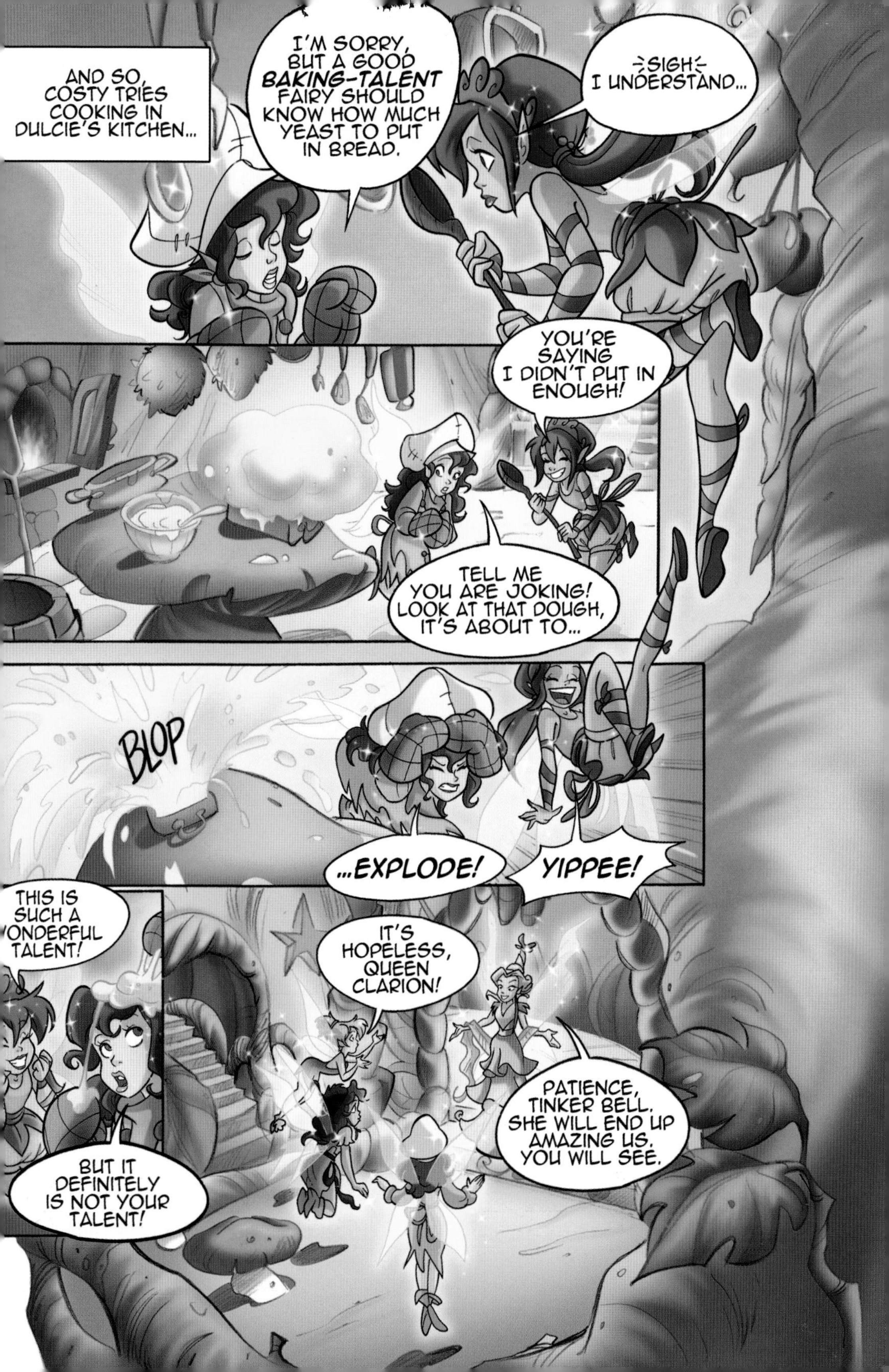
AND SO, COSTY TRIES COOKING IN DULCIE'S KITCHEN...
I'M SORRY, BUT A GOOD BAKING-TALENT FAIRY SHOULD KNOW HOW MUCH YEAST TO PUT IN BREAD.
SIGH I UNDERSTAND...
YOU'RE SAYING I DIDN'T PUT IN ENOUGH!
TELL ME YOU ARE JOKING! LOOK AT THAT DOUGH, IT'S ABOUT TO...
BLOP
...EXPLODE!
YIPPEE!
THIS IS SUCH A WONDERFUL TALENT!
BUT IT DEFINITELY IS NOT YOUR TALENT!
IT'S HOPELESS, QUEEN CLARION!
PATIENCE, TINKER BELL. SHE WILL END UP AMAZING US. YOU WILL SEE.

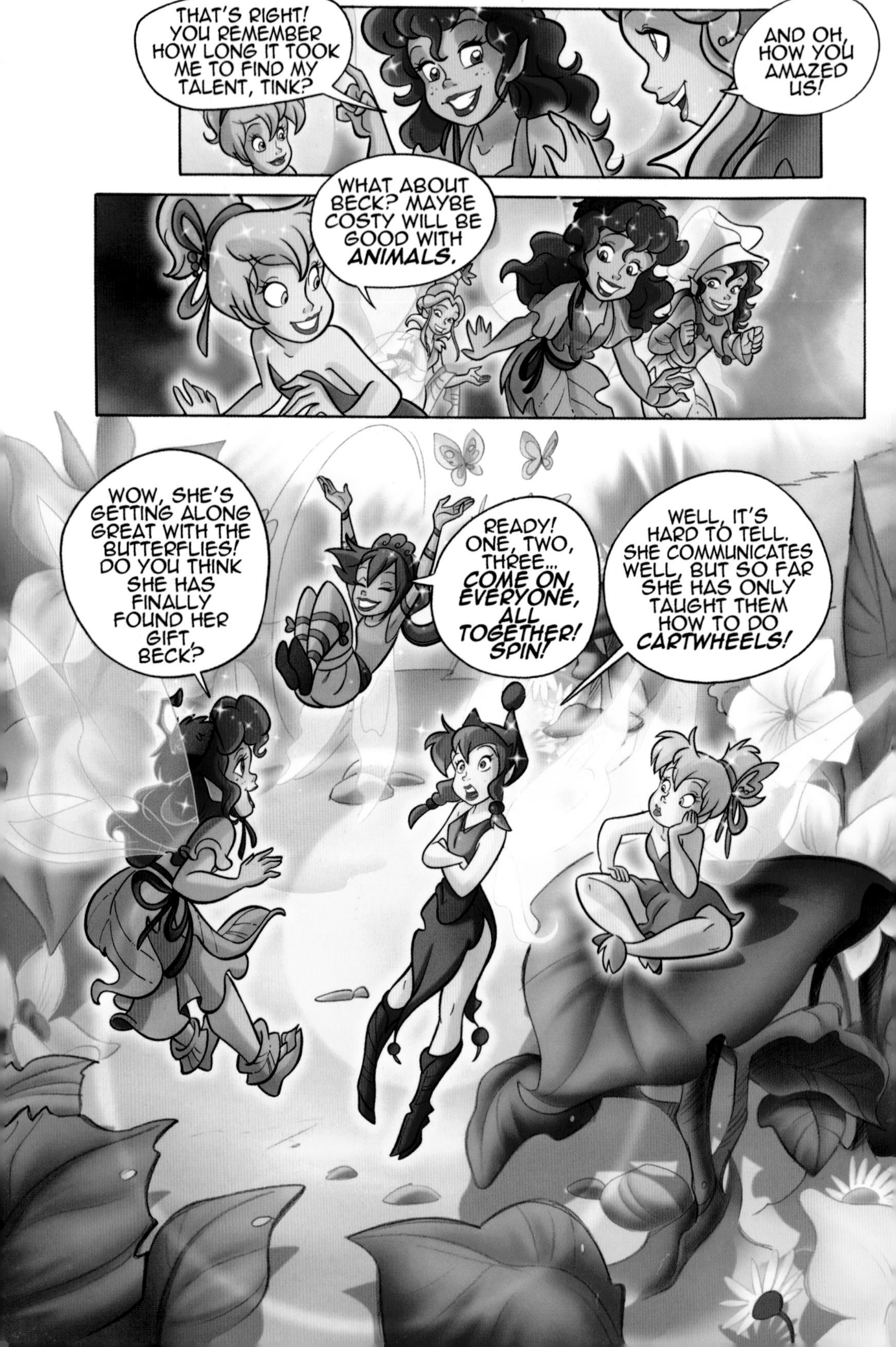
THAT'S RIGHT! YOU REMEMBER HOW LONG IT TOOK ME TO FIND MY TALENT, TINK?
AND OH, HOW YOU AMAZED US!
WHAT ABOUT BECK? MAYBE COSTY WILL BE GOOD WITH **ANIMALS.**
WOW, SHE'S GETTING ALONG GREAT WITH THE BUTTERFLIES! DO YOU THINK SHE HAS FINALLY FOUND HER GIFT, BECK?
READY! ONE, TWO, THREE... ***COME ON, EVERYONE, ALL TOGETHER! SPIN!***
WELL, IT'S HARD TO TELL. SHE COMMUNICATES WELL, BUT SO FAR SHE HAS ONLY TAUGHT THEM HOW TO DO **CARTWHEELS!**

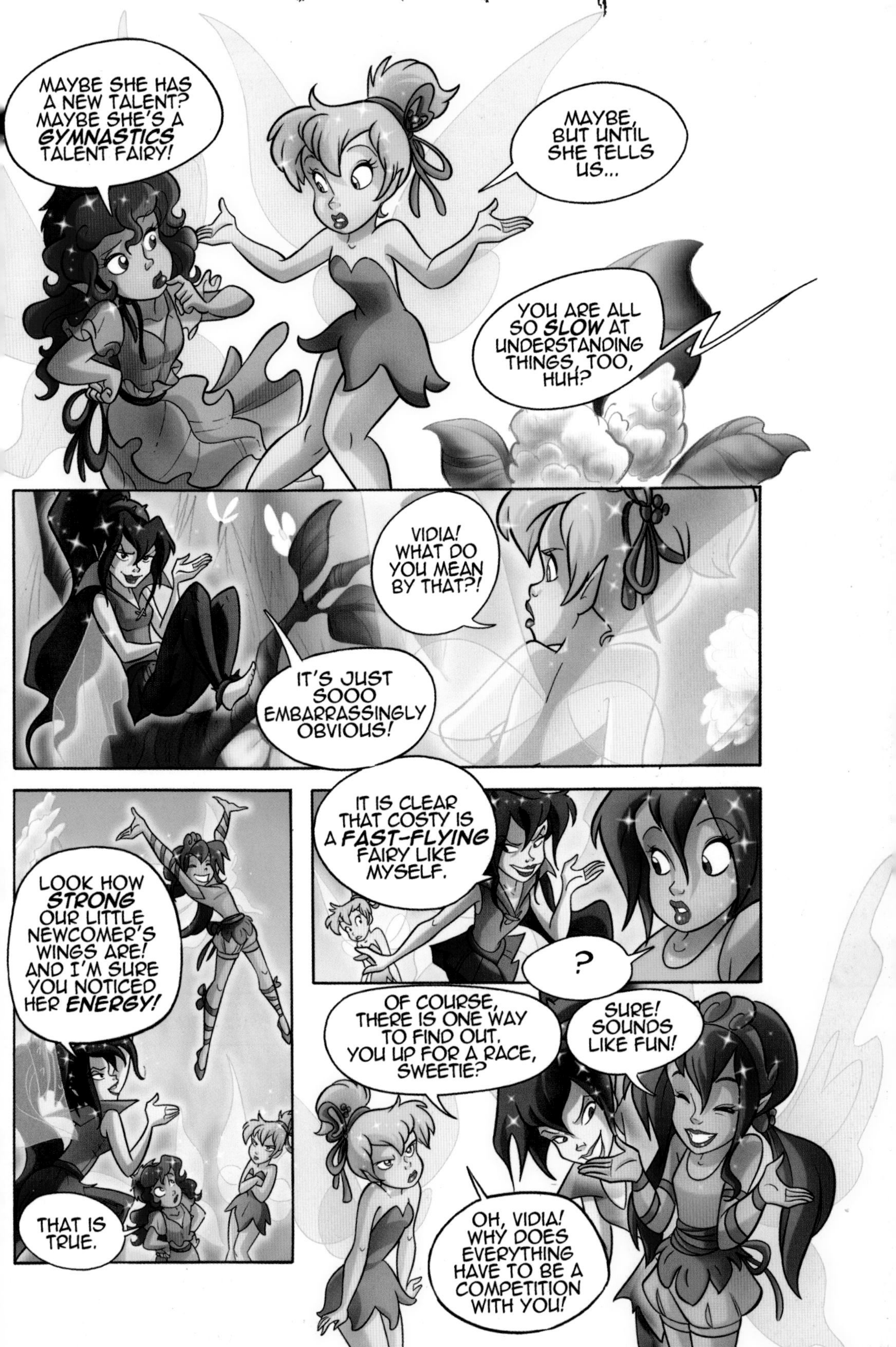
MAYBE SHE HAS A NEW TALENT? MAYBE SHE'S A *GYMNASTICS* TALENT FAIRY!
MAYBE, BUT UNTIL SHE TELLS US...
YOU ARE ALL SO **SLOW** AT UNDERSTANDING THINGS, TOO, HUH?
VIDIA! WHAT DO YOU MEAN BY THAT?!
IT'S JUST SOOO EMBARRASSINGLY OBVIOUS!
LOOK HOW **STRONG** OUR LITTLE NEWCOMER'S WINGS ARE! AND I'M SURE YOU NOTICED HER **ENERGY!**
THAT IS TRUE.
IT IS CLEAR THAT COSTY IS A **FAST-FLYING** FAIRY LIKE MYSELF.
?
OF COURSE, THERE IS ONE WAY TO FIND OUT. YOU UP FOR A RACE, SWEETIE?
SURE! SOUNDS LIKE FUN!
OH, VIDIA! WHY DOES EVERYTHING HAVE TO BE A COMPETITION WITH YOU!

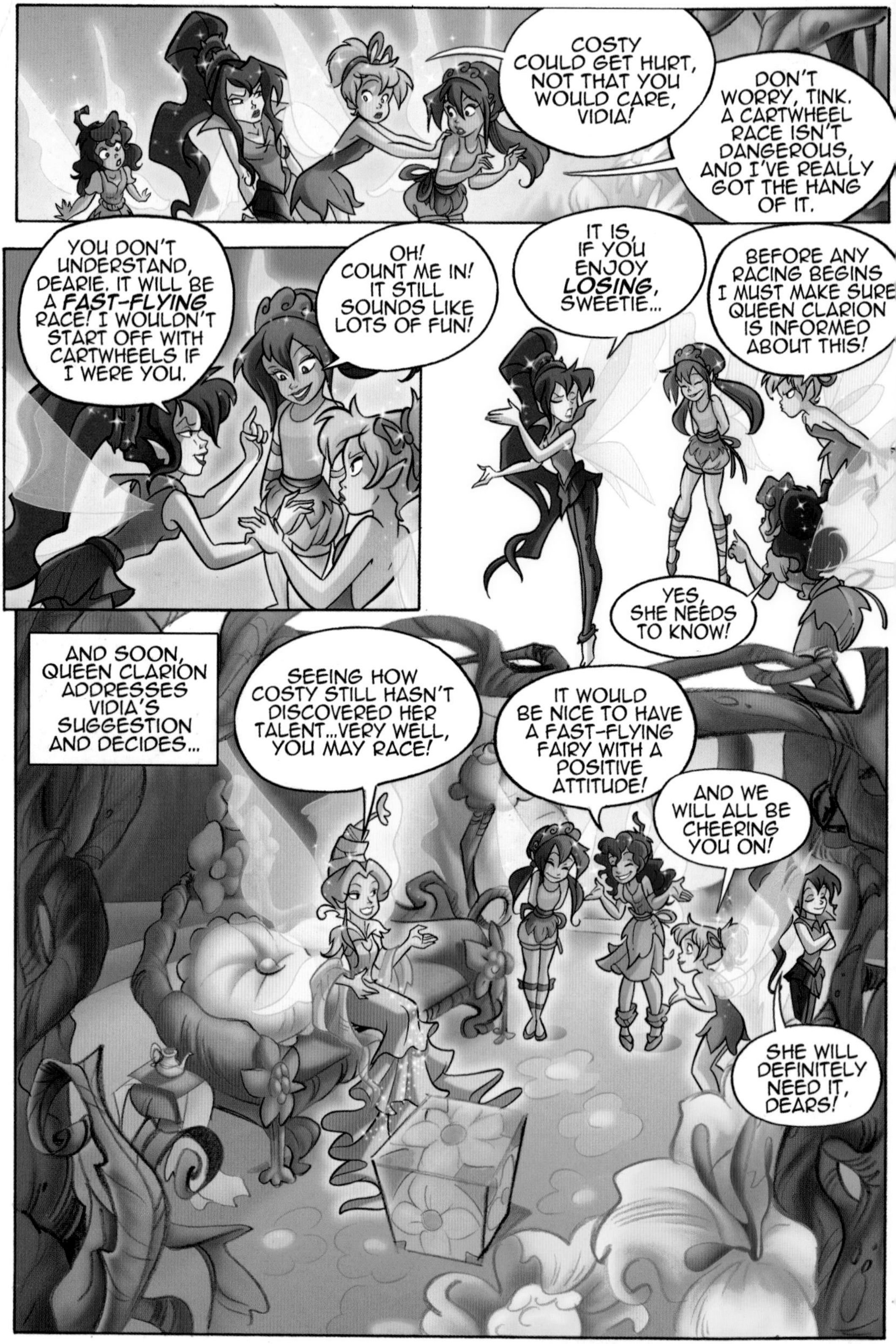
COSTY COULD GET HURT, NOT THAT YOU WOULD CARE, VIDIA!
DON'T WORRY, TINK. A CARTWHEEL RACE ISN'T DANGEROUS, AND I'VE REALLY GOT THE HANG OF IT.
YOU DON'T UNDERSTAND, DEARIE. IT WILL BE A FAST-FLYING RACE! I WOULDN'T START OFF WITH CARTWHEELS IF I WERE YOU.
OH! COUNT ME IN! IT STILL SOUNDS LIKE LOTS OF FUN!
IT IS, IF YOU ENJOY LOSING, SWEETIE...
BEFORE ANY RACING BEGINS I MUST MAKE SURE QUEEN CLARION IS INFORMED ABOUT THIS!
YES, SHE NEEDS TO KNOW!
AND SOON, QUEEN CLARION ADDRESSES VIDIA'S SUGGESTION AND DECIDES...
SEEING HOW COSTY STILL HASN'T DISCOVERED HER TALENT...VERY WELL, YOU MAY RACE!
IT WOULD BE NICE TO HAVE A FAST-FLYING FAIRY WITH A POSITIVE ATTITUDE!
AND WE WILL ALL BE CHEERING YOU ON!
SHE WILL DEFINITELY NEED IT, DEARS!

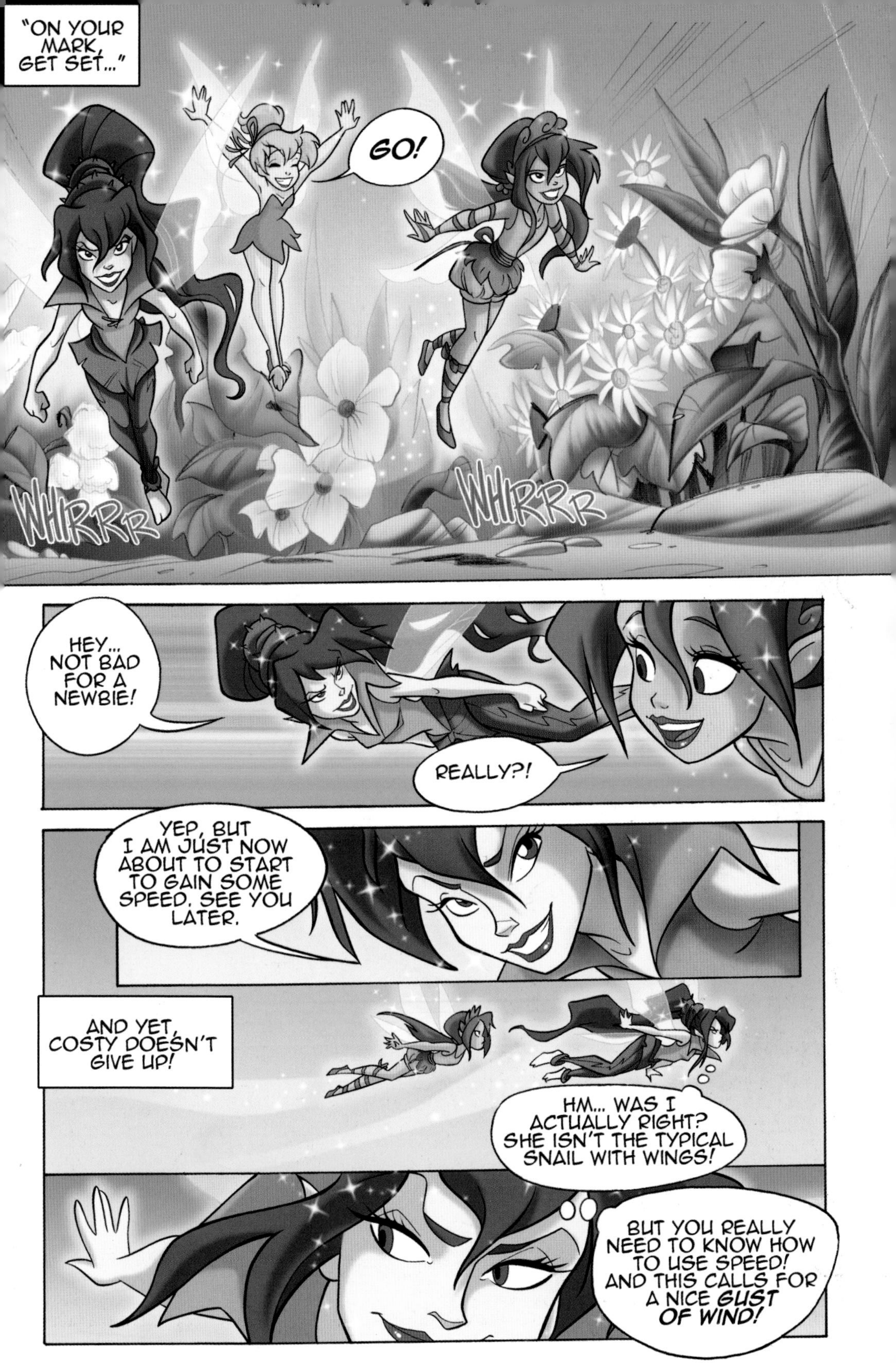
"ON YOUR MARK, GET SET..."
GO!
WHIRRR
WHIRRR
HEY... NOT BAD FOR A NEWBIE!
REALLY?!
YEP, BUT I AM JUST NOW ABOUT TO START TO GAIN SOME SPEED. SEE YOU LATER.
AND YET, COSTY DOESN'T GIVE UP!
HM... WAS I ACTUALLY RIGHT? SHE ISN'T THE TYPICAL SNAIL WITH WINGS!
BUT YOU REALLY NEED TO KNOW HOW TO USE SPEED! AND THIS CALLS FOR A NICE GUST OF WIND!

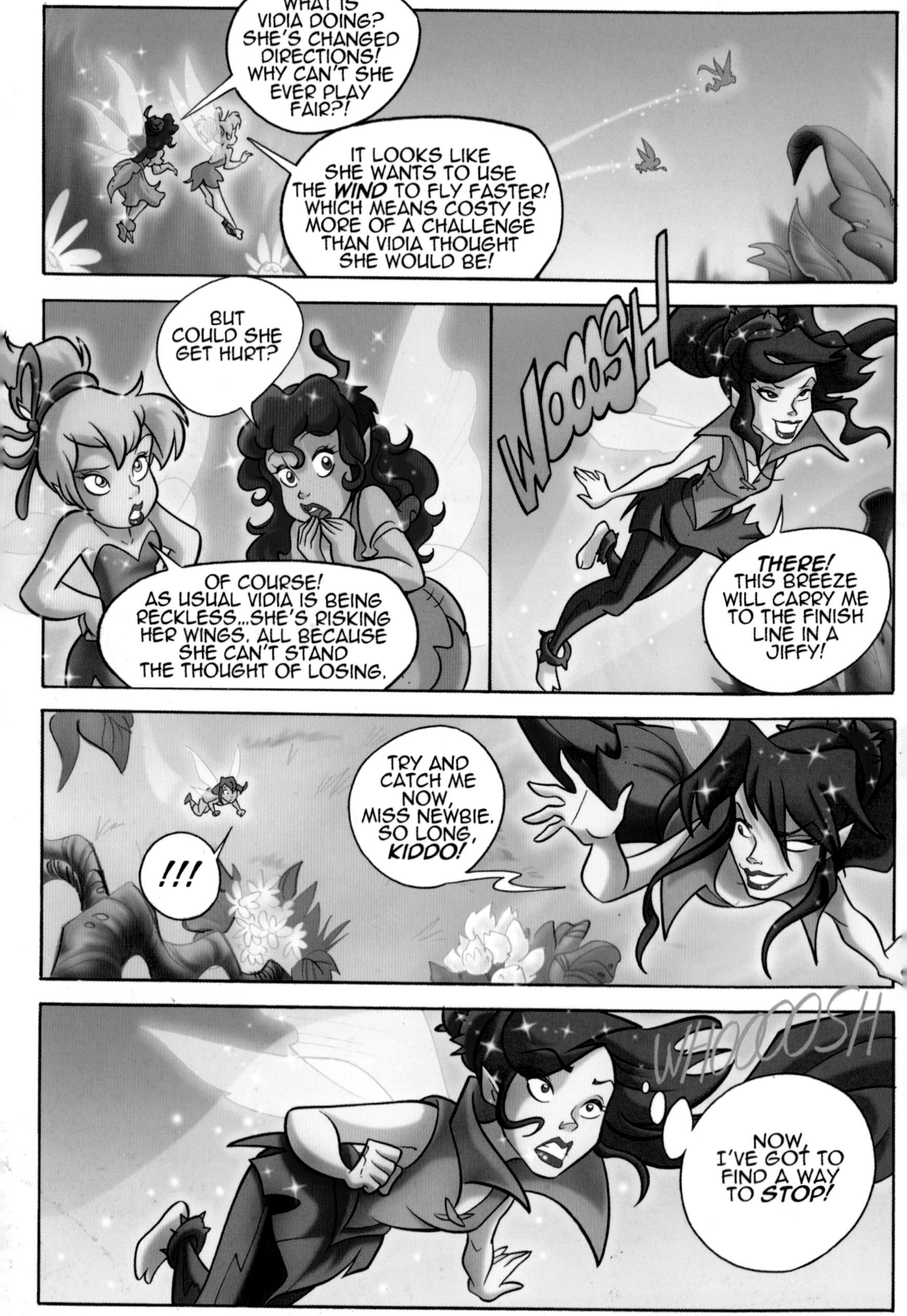
WHAT IS VIDIA DOING? SHE'S CHANGED DIRECTIONS! WHY CAN'T SHE EVER PLAY FAIR?!
IT LOOKS LIKE SHE WANTS TO USE THE WIND TO FLY FASTER! WHICH MEANS COSTY IS MORE OF A CHALLENGE THAN VIDIA THOUGHT SHE WOULD BE!
BUT COULD SHE GET HURT?
OF COURSE! AS USUAL VIDIA IS BEING RECKLESS...SHE'S RISKING HER WINGS, ALL BECAUSE SHE CAN'T STAND THE THOUGHT OF LOSING.
WOOOSH
THERE! THIS BREEZE WILL CARRY ME TO THE FINISH LINE IN A JIFFY!
TRY AND CATCH ME NOW, MISS NEWBIE. SO LONG, KIDDO!
!!!
WHOOOOSH
NOW, I'VE GOT TO FIND A WAY TO STOP!

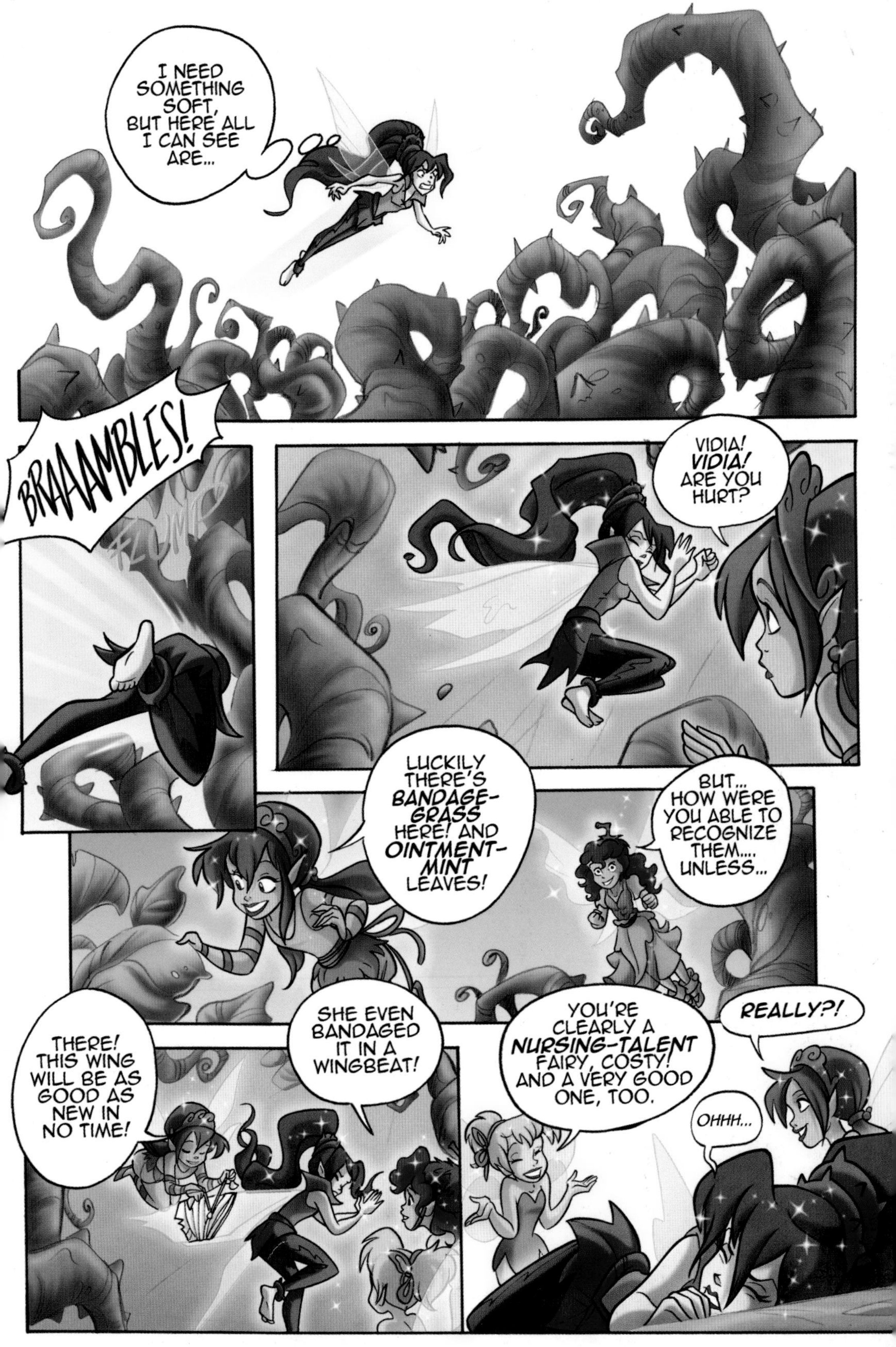
I NEED SOMETHING SOFT, BUT HERE ALL I CAN SEE ARE...
BRAAAMBLES!
FLUMP
VIDIA! VIDIA! ARE YOU HURT?
LUCKILY THERE'S BANDAGE-GRASS HERE! AND OINTMENT-MINT LEAVES!
BUT... HOW WERE YOU ABLE TO RECOGNIZE THEM.... UNLESS...
THERE! THIS WING WILL BE AS GOOD AS NEW IN NO TIME!
SHE EVEN BANDAGED IT IN A WINGBEAT!
YOU'RE CLEARLY A NURSING-TALENT FAIRY, COSTY! AND A VERY GOOD ONE, TOO.
REALLY?!
OHHH...

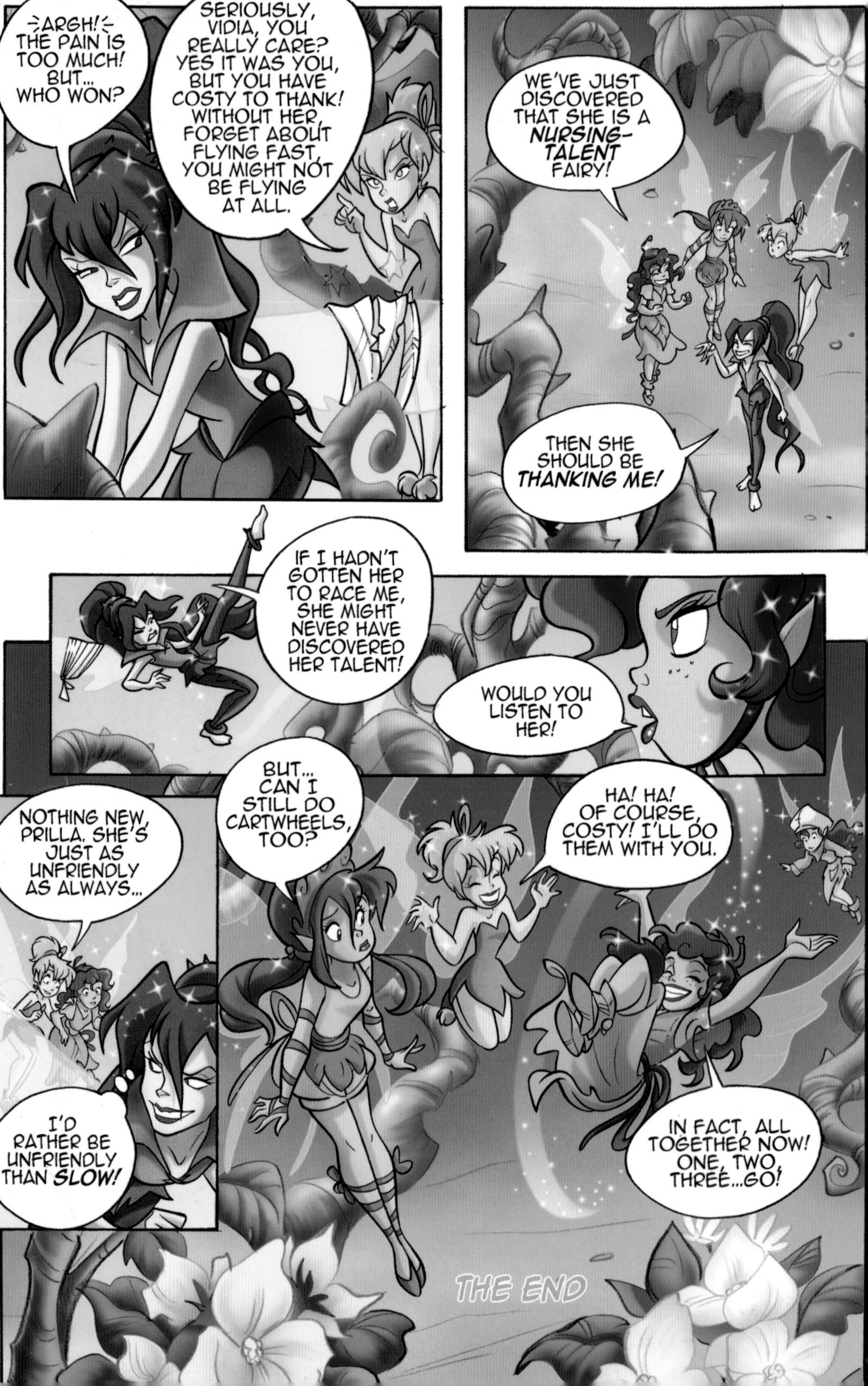

ARGH! THE PAIN IS TOO MUCH! BUT... WHO WON?
SERIOUSLY, VIDIA, YOU REALLY CARE? YES IT WAS YOU, BUT YOU HAVE COSTY TO THANK! WITHOUT HER, FORGET ABOUT FLYING FAST, YOU MIGHT NOT BE FLYING AT ALL.
WE'VE JUST DISCOVERED THAT SHE IS A ***NURSING-TALENT*** FAIRY!
THEN SHE SHOULD BE ***THANKING ME!***
IF I HADN'T GOTTEN HER TO RACE ME, SHE MIGHT NEVER HAVE DISCOVERED HER TALENT!
WOULD YOU LISTEN TO HER!
NOTHING NEW, PRILLA. SHE'S JUST AS UNFRIENDLY AS ALWAYS...
I'D RATHER BE UNFRIENDLY THAN ***SLOW!***
BUT... CAN I STILL DO CARTWHEELS, TOO?
HA! HA! OF COURSE, COSTY! I'LL DO THEM WITH YOU.
IN FACT, ALL TOGETHER NOW! ONE, TWO, THREE...GO!
THE END

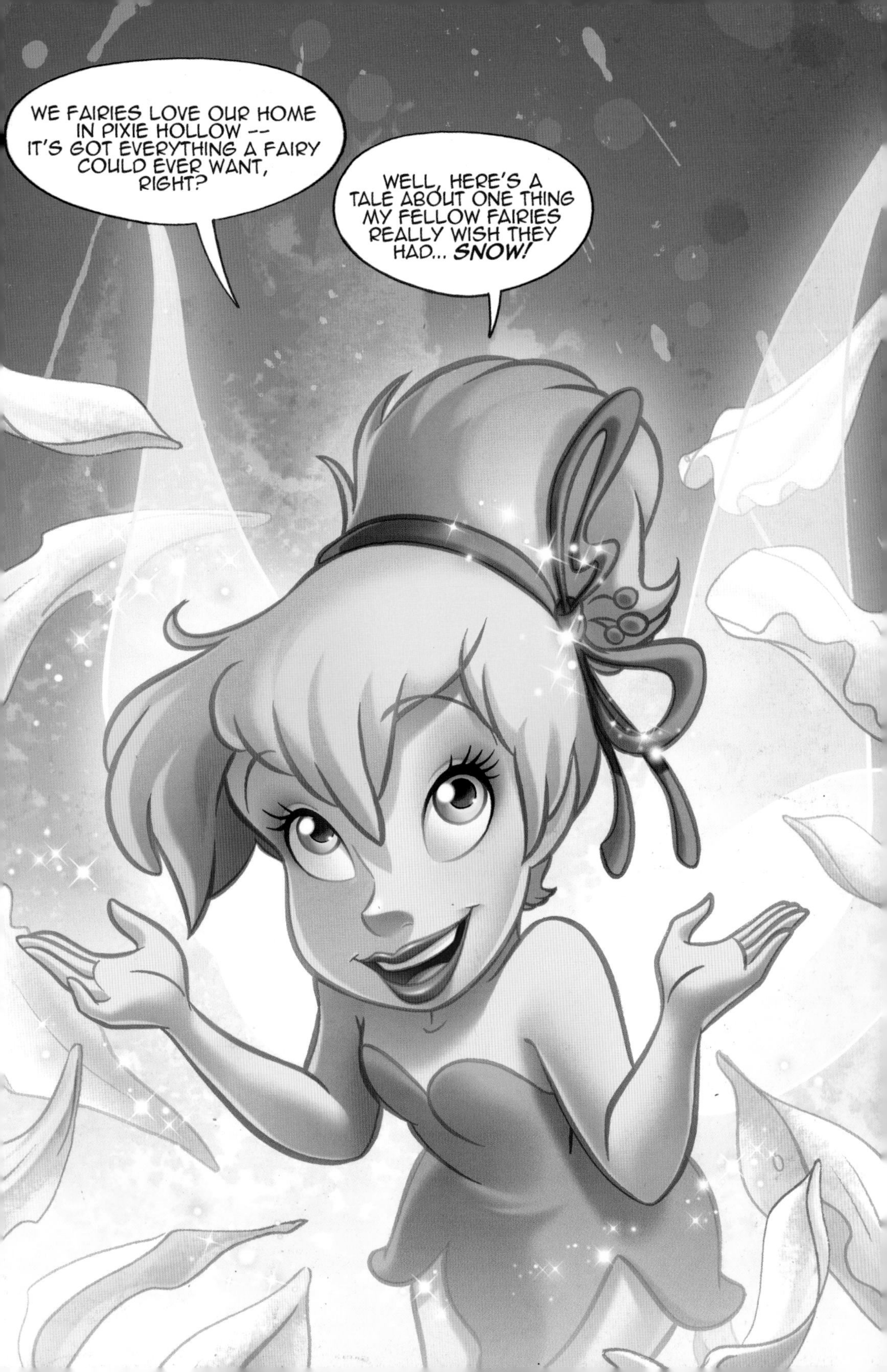
WE FAIRIES LOVE OUR HOME IN PIXIE HOLLOW -- IT'S GOT EVERYTHING A FAIRY COULD EVER WANT, RIGHT?
WELL, HERE'S A TALE ABOUT ONE THING MY FELLOW FAIRIES REALLY WISH THEY HAD... *SNOW!*

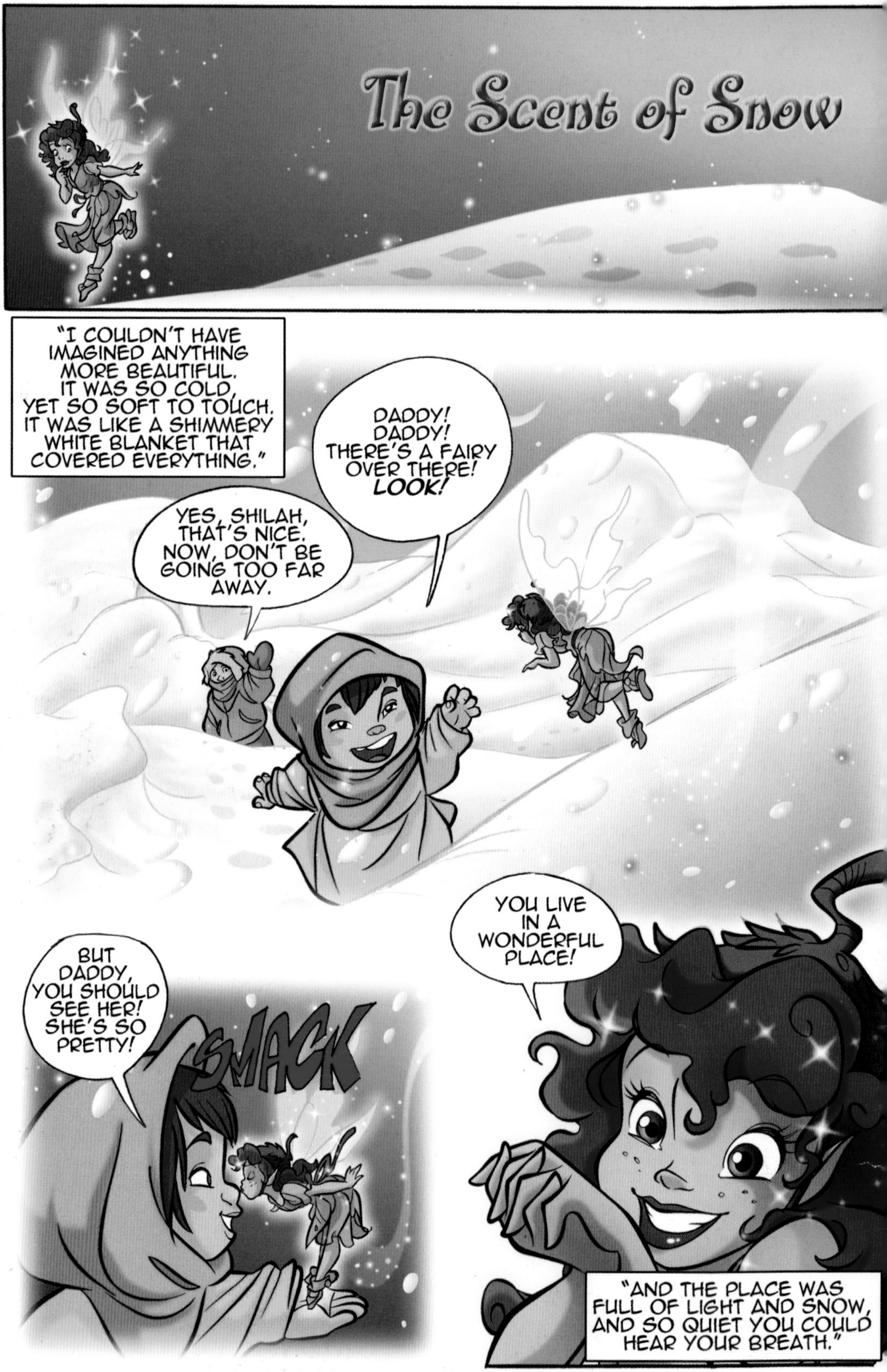

The Scent of Snow
"I COULDN'T HAVE IMAGINED ANYTHING MORE BEAUTIFUL. IT WAS SO COLD, YET SO SOFT TO TOUCH. IT WAS LIKE A SHIMMERY WHITE BLANKET THAT COVERED EVERYTHING."
DADDY! DADDY! THERE'S A FAIRY OVER THERE! LOOK!
YES, SHILAH, THAT'S NICE. NOW, DON'T BE GOING TOO FAR AWAY.
BUT DADDY, YOU SHOULD SEE HER! SHE'S SO PRETTY!
SMACK
YOU LIVE IN A WONDERFUL PLACE!
"AND THE PLACE WAS FULL OF LIGHT AND SNOW, AND SO QUIET YOU COULD HEAR YOUR BREATH."

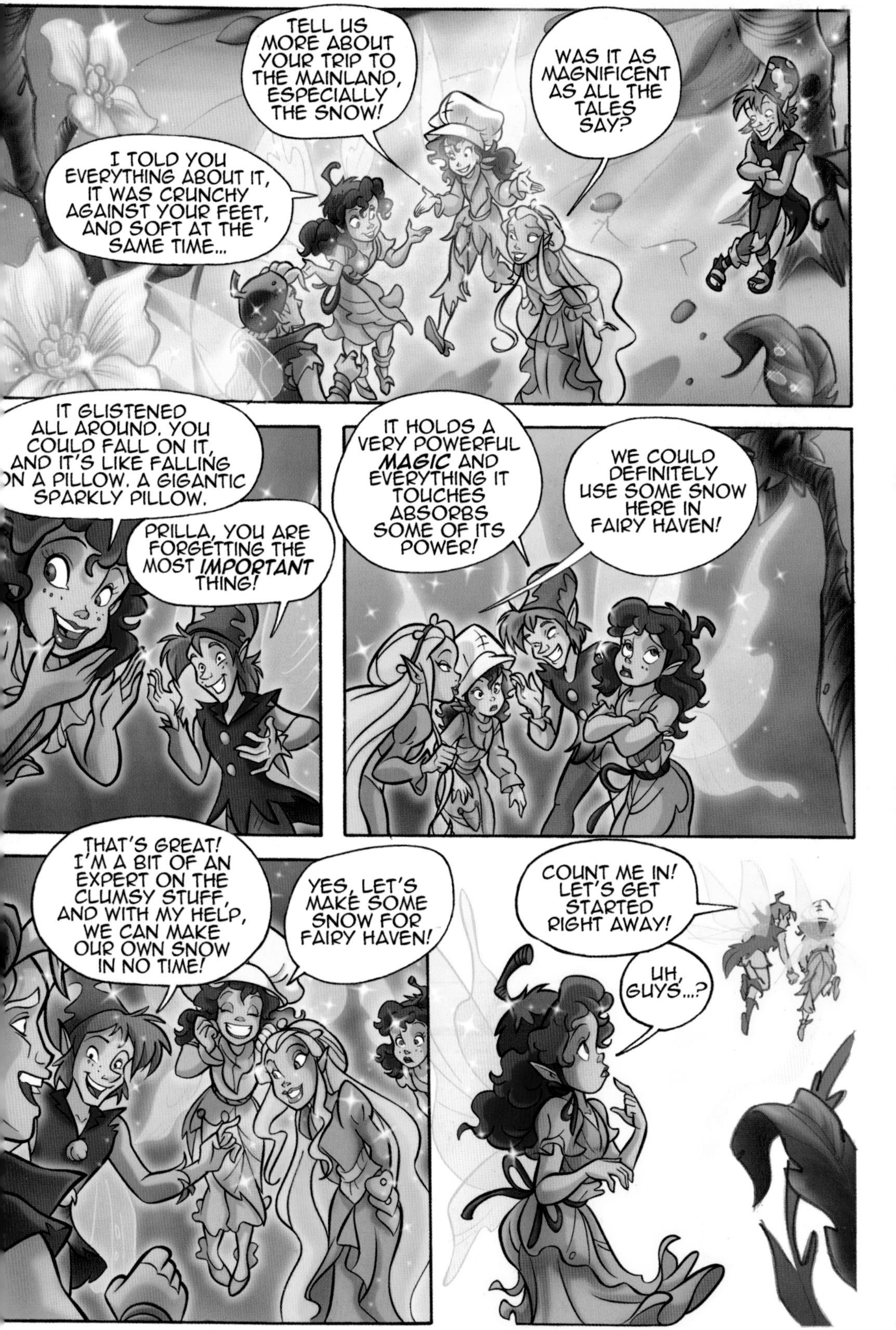

TELL US MORE ABOUT YOUR TRIP TO THE MAINLAND, ESPECIALLY THE SNOW!
WAS IT AS MAGNIFICENT AS ALL THE TALES SAY?
I TOLD YOU EVERYTHING ABOUT IT, IT WAS CRUNCHY AGAINST YOUR FEET, AND SOFT AT THE SAME TIME...
IT GLISTENED ALL AROUND. YOU COULD FALL ON IT, AND IT'S LIKE FALLING ON A PILLOW. A GIGANTIC SPARKLY PILLOW.
PRILLA, YOU ARE FORGETTING THE MOST *IMPORTANT* THING!
IT HOLDS A VERY POWERFUL *MAGIC* AND EVERYTHING IT TOUCHES ABSORBS SOME OF ITS POWER!
WE COULD DEFINITELY USE SOME SNOW HERE IN FAIRY HAVEN!
THAT'S GREAT! I'M A BIT OF AN EXPERT ON THE CLUMSY STUFF, AND WITH MY HELP, WE CAN MAKE OUR OWN SNOW IN NO TIME!
YES, LET'S MAKE SOME SNOW FOR FAIRY HAVEN!
COUNT ME IN! LET'S GET STARTED RIGHT AWAY!
UH, GUYS...?

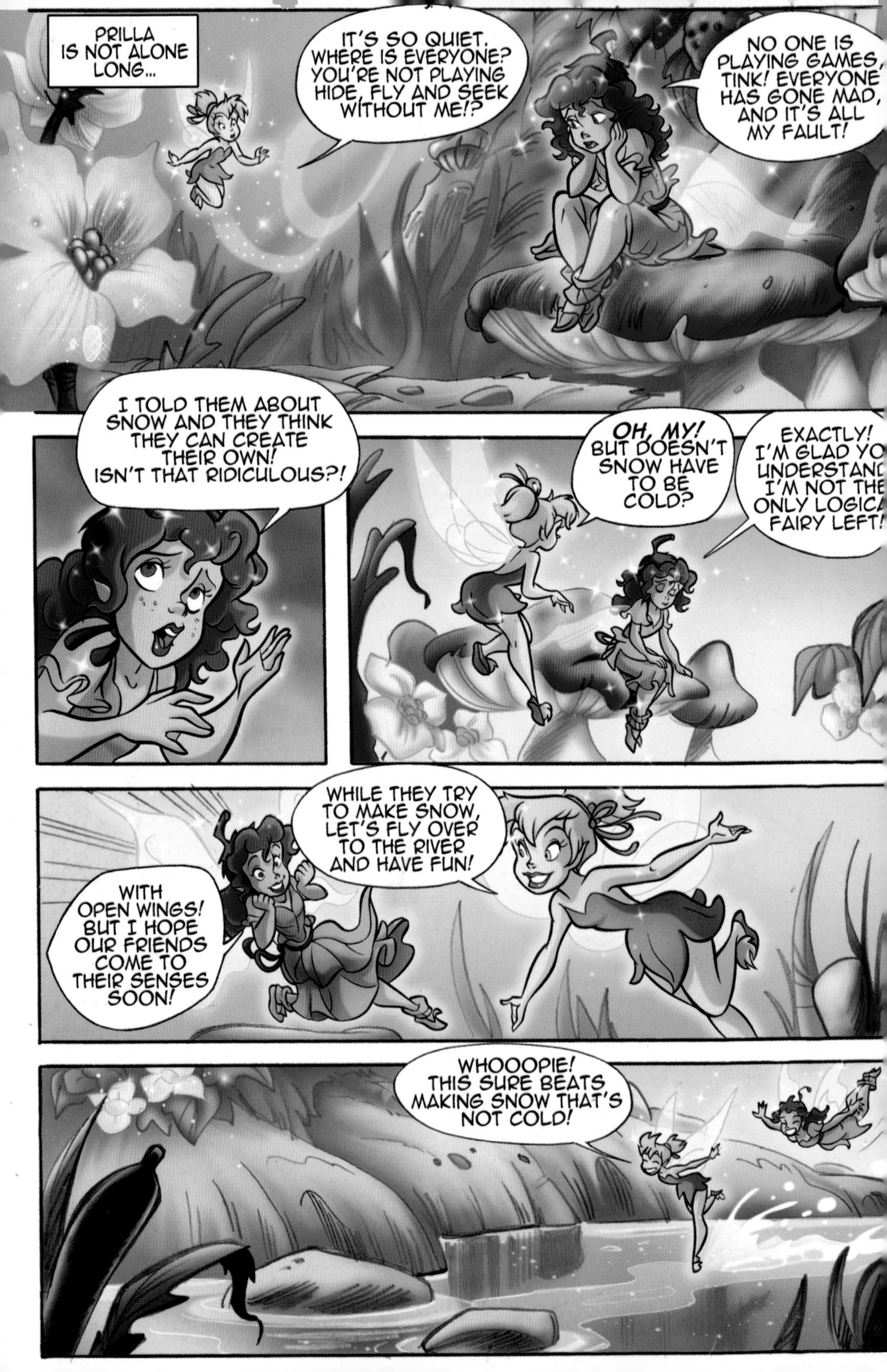
PRILLA IS NOT ALONE LONG...
IT'S SO QUIET. WHERE IS EVERYONE? YOU'RE NOT PLAYING HIDE, FLY AND SEEK WITHOUT ME!?
NO ONE IS PLAYING GAMES, TINK! EVERYONE HAS GONE MAD, AND IT'S ALL MY FAULT!
I TOLD THEM ABOUT SNOW AND THEY THINK THEY CAN CREATE THEIR OWN! ISN'T THAT RIDICULOUS?!
OH, MY! BUT DOESN'T SNOW HAVE TO BE COLD?
EXACTLY! I'M GLAD YO UNDERSTAND I'M NOT THE ONLY LOGIC FAIRY LEFT!
WHILE THEY TRY TO MAKE SNOW, LET'S FLY OVER TO THE RIVER AND HAVE FUN!
WITH OPEN WINGS! BUT I HOPE OUR FRIENDS COME TO THEIR SENSES SOON!
WHOOOPIE! THIS SURE BEATS MAKING SNOW THAT'S NOT COLD!

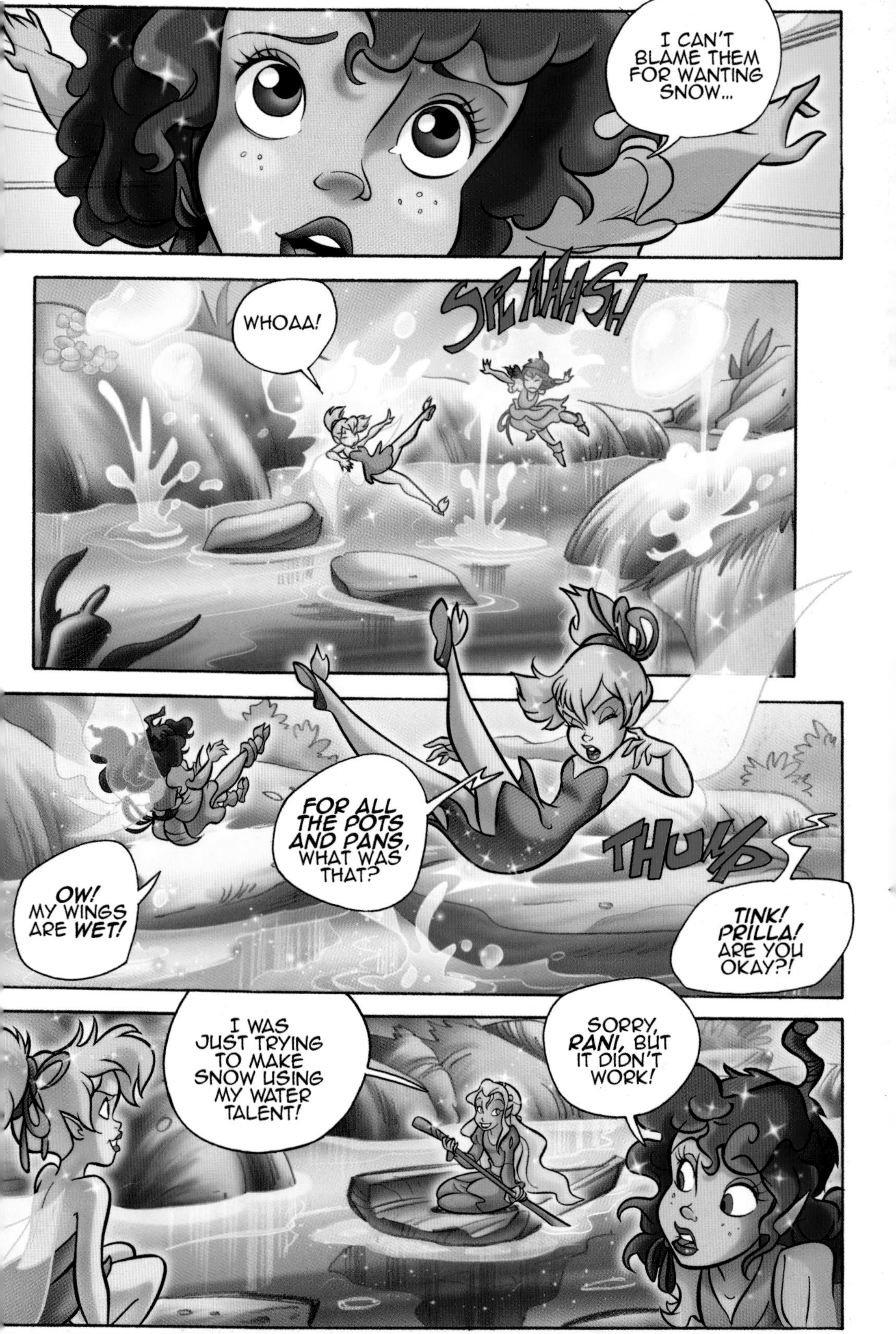
I CAN'T BLAME THEM FOR WANTING SNOW...
WHOAA!
SPLAAASH
FOR ALL THE POTS AND PANS, WHAT WAS THAT?
THUMP
OW! MY WINGS ARE WET!
TINK! PRILLA! ARE YOU OKAY?!
I WAS JUST TRYING TO MAKE SNOW USING MY WATER TALENT!
SORRY, RANI, BUT IT DIDN'T WORK!

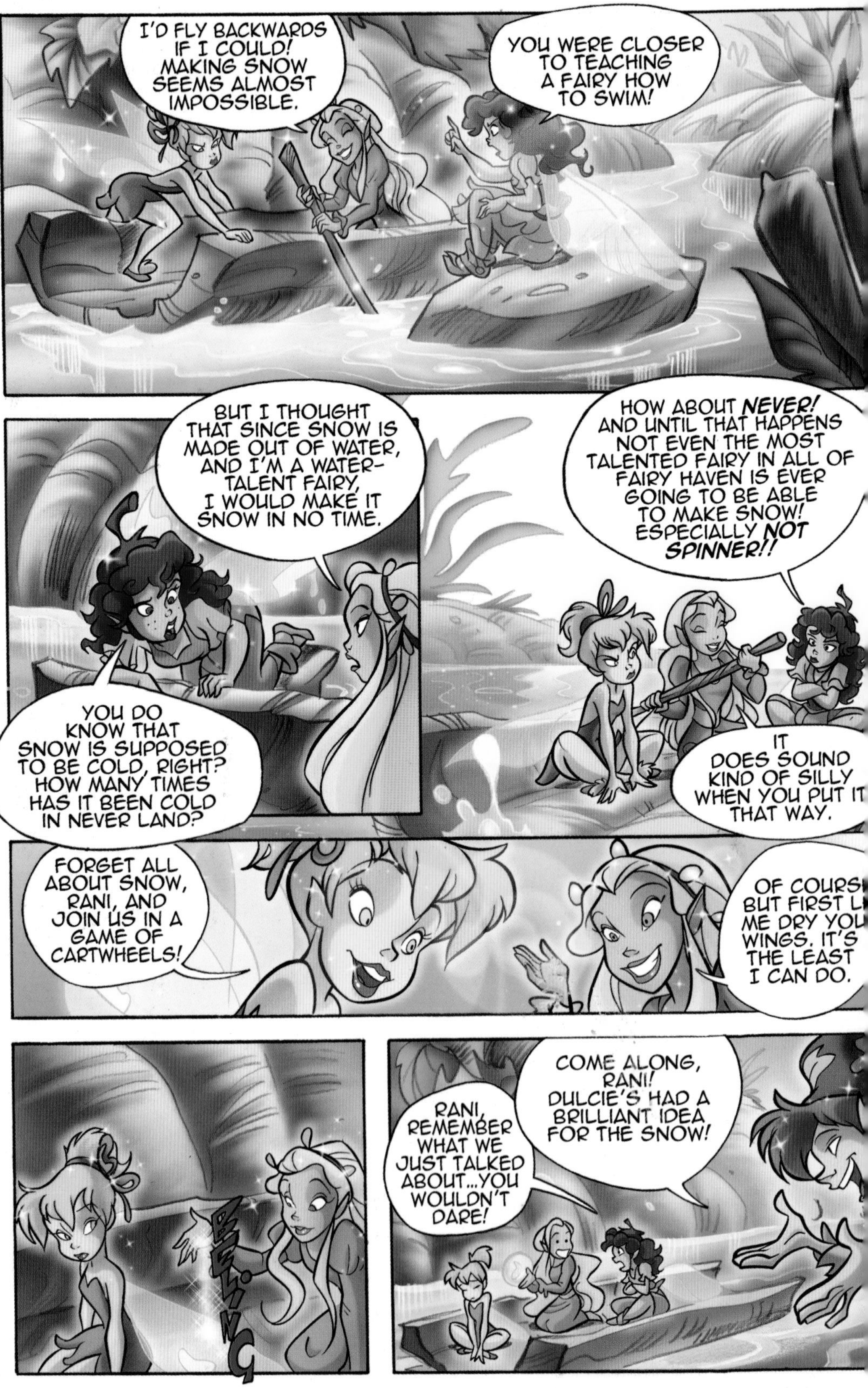

I'D FLY BACKWARDS IF I COULD! MAKING SNOW SEEMS ALMOST IMPOSSIBLE.
YOU WERE CLOSER TO TEACHING A FAIRY HOW TO SWIM!
BUT I THOUGHT THAT SINCE SNOW IS MADE OUT OF WATER, AND I'M A WATER-TALENT FAIRY, I WOULD MAKE IT SNOW IN NO TIME.
YOU DO KNOW THAT SNOW IS SUPPOSED TO BE COLD, RIGHT? HOW MANY TIMES HAS IT BEEN COLD IN NEVER LAND?
HOW ABOUT NEVER! AND UNTIL THAT HAPPENS NOT EVEN THE MOST TALENTED FAIRY IN ALL OF FAIRY HAVEN IS EVER GOING TO BE ABLE TO MAKE SNOW! ESPECIALLY NOT SPINNER!!
IT DOES SOUND KIND OF SILLY WHEN YOU PUT IT THAT WAY.
FORGET ALL ABOUT SNOW, RANI, AND JOIN US IN A GAME OF CARTWHEELS!
OF COURS BUT FIRST L ME DRY YOU WINGS. IT'S THE LEAST I CAN DO.
BEE-LING
COME ALONG, RANI! DULCIE'S HAD A BRILLIANT IDEA FOR THE SNOW!
RANI, REMEMBER WHAT WE JUST TALKED ABOUT...YOU WOULDN'T DARE!

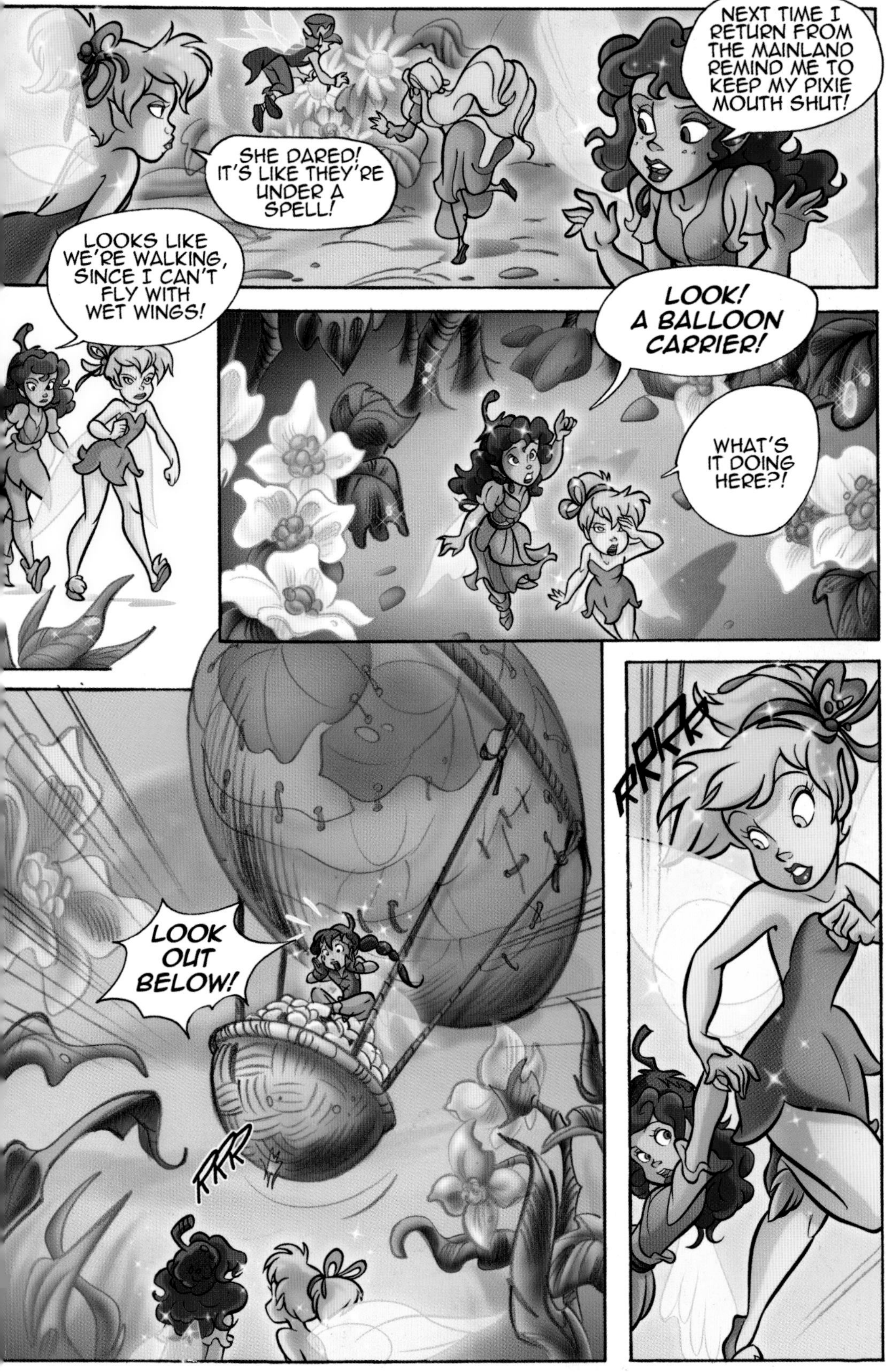
SHE DARED! IT'S LIKE THEY'RE UNDER A SPELL!
NEXT TIME I RETURN FROM THE MAINLAND REMIND ME TO KEEP MY PIXIE MOUTH SHUT!
LOOKS LIKE WE'RE WALKING, SINCE I CAN'T FLY WITH WET WINGS!
LOOK! A BALLOON CARRIER!
WHAT'S IT DOING HERE?!
LOOK OUT BELOW!
RRR
RRRR

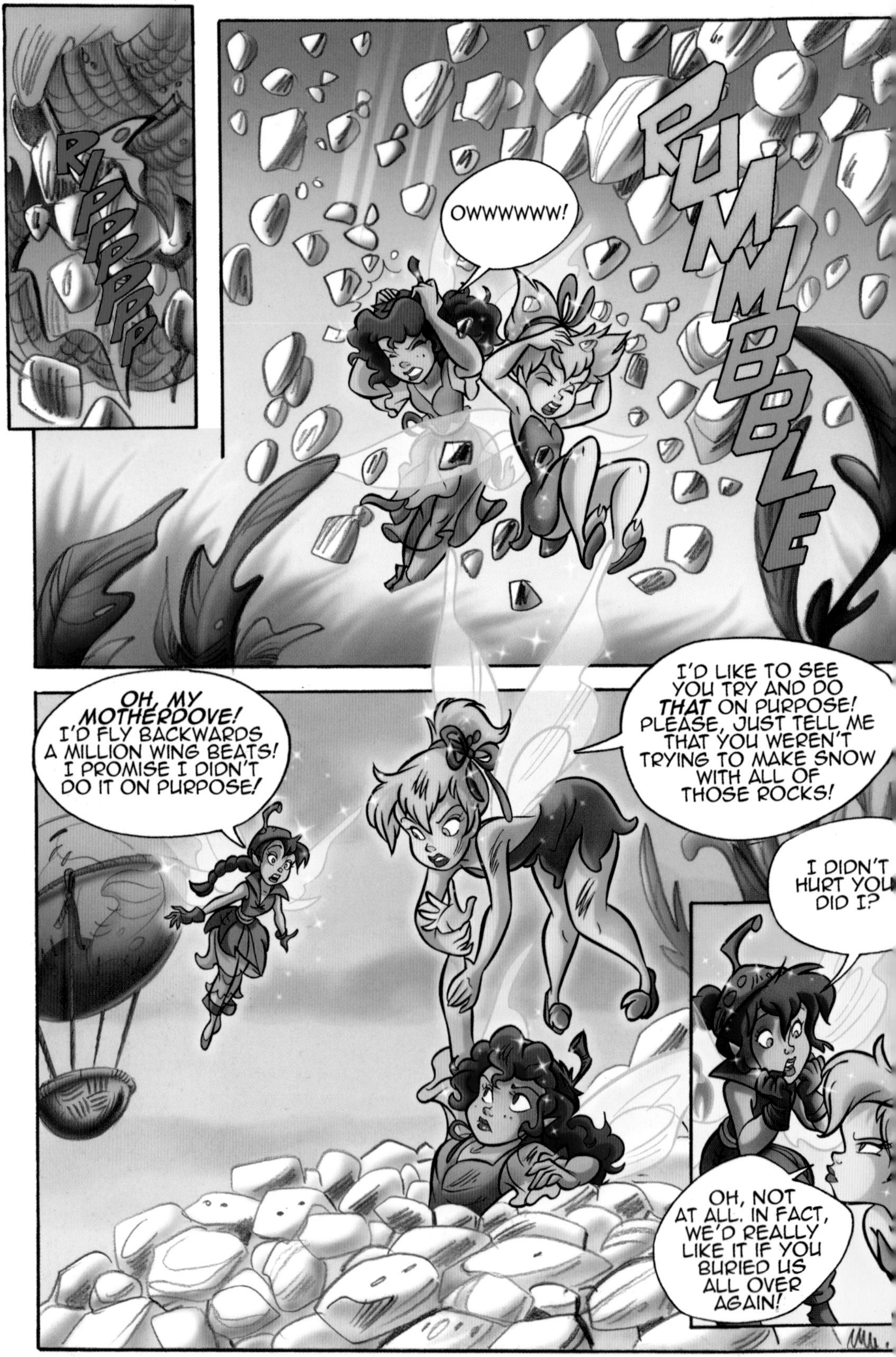
RIPPPPPP
RUMMBBLE
OWWWWWW!
OH, MY MOTHERDOVE! I'D FLY BACKWARDS A MILLION WING BEATS! I PROMISE I DIDN'T DO IT ON PURPOSE!
I'D LIKE TO SEE YOU TRY AND DO THAT ON PURPOSE! PLEASE, JUST TELL ME THAT YOU WEREN'T TRYING TO MAKE SNOW WITH ALL OF THOSE ROCKS!
I DIDN'T HURT YOU DID I?
OH, NOT AT ALL. IN FACT, WE'D REALLY LIKE IT IF YOU BURIED US ALL OVER AGAIN!

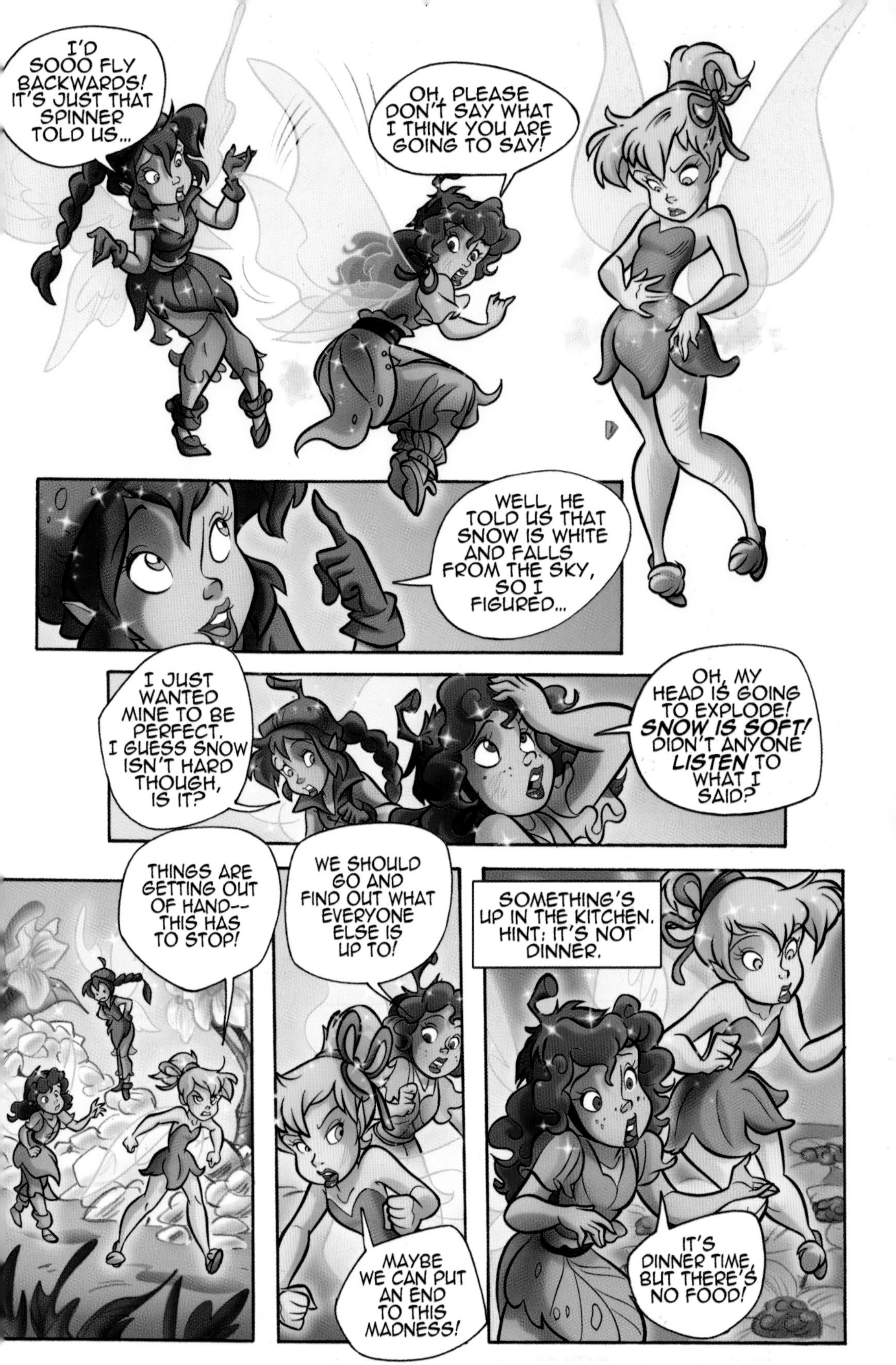
I'D SOOO FLY BACKWARDS! IT'S JUST THAT SPINNER TOLD US...
OH, PLEASE DON'T SAY WHAT I THINK YOU ARE GOING TO SAY!
WELL, HE TOLD US THAT SNOW IS WHITE AND FALLS FROM THE SKY, SO I FIGURED...
I JUST WANTED MINE TO BE PERFECT. I GUESS SNOW ISN'T HARD THOUGH, IS IT?
OH, MY HEAD IS GOING TO EXPLODE! SNOW IS SOFT! DIDN'T ANYONE LISTEN TO WHAT I SAID?
THINGS ARE GETTING OUT OF HAND-- THIS HAS TO STOP!
WE SHOULD GO AND FIND OUT WHAT EVERYONE ELSE IS UP TO!
MAYBE WE CAN PUT AN END TO THIS MADNESS!
SOMETHING'S UP IN THE KITCHEN. HINT: IT'S NOT DINNER.
IT'S DINNER TIME, BUT THERE'S NO FOOD!

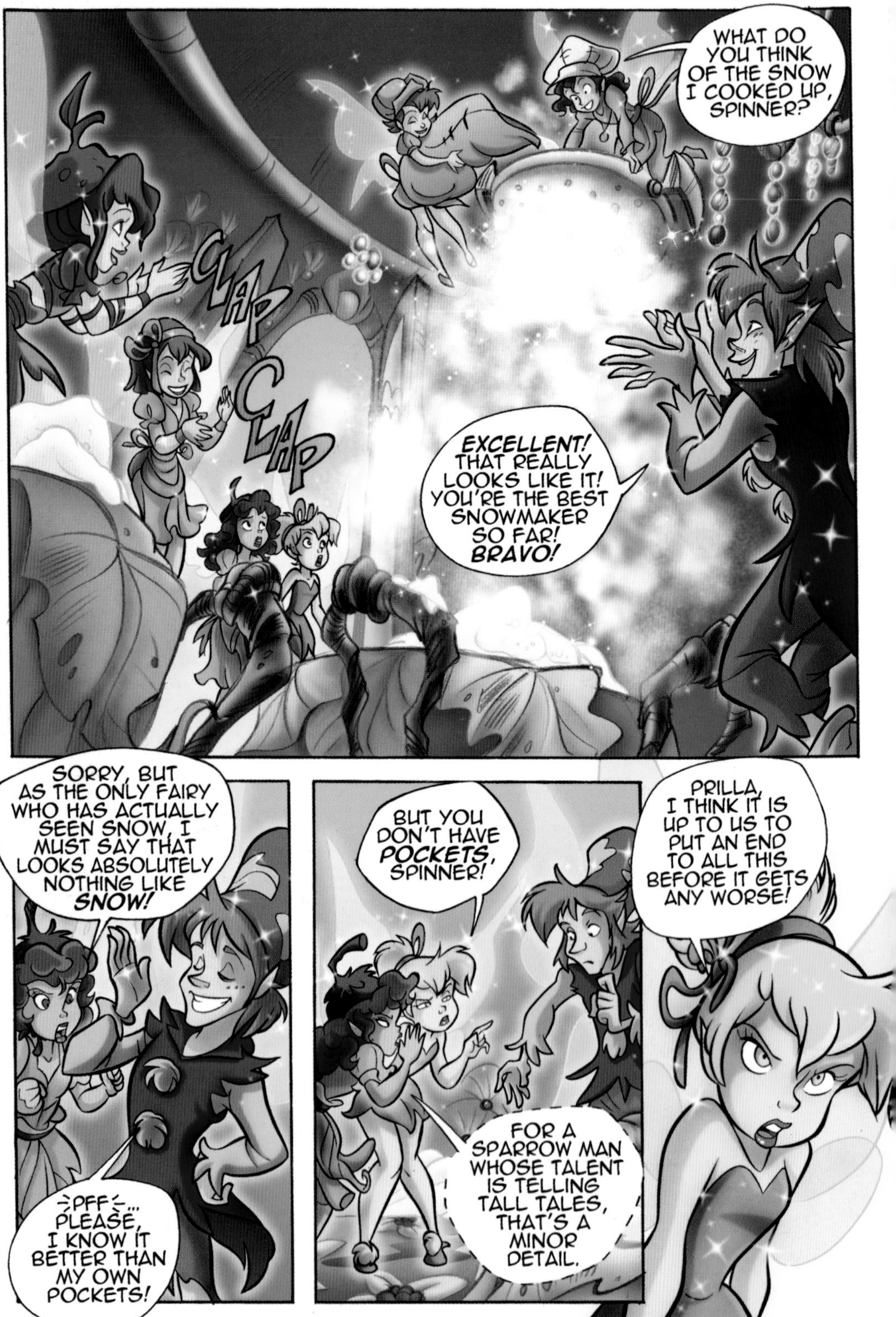
WHAT DO YOU THINK OF THE SNOW I COOKED UP, SPINNER?
CLAP
CLAP
EXCELLENT! THAT REALLY LOOKS LIKE IT! YOU'RE THE BEST SNOWMAKER SO FAR! BRAVO!
SORRY, BUT AS THE ONLY FAIRY WHO HAS ACTUALLY SEEN SNOW, I MUST SAY THAT LOOKS ABSOLUTELY NOTHING LIKE SNOW!
PFF... PLEASE, I KNOW IT BETTER THAN MY OWN POCKETS!
BUT YOU DON'T HAVE POCKETS, SPINNER!
FOR A SPARROW MAN WHOSE TALENT IS TELLING TALL TALES, THAT'S A MINOR DETAIL.
PRILLA, I THINK IT IS UP TO US TO PUT AN END TO ALL THIS BEFORE IT GETS ANY WORSE!

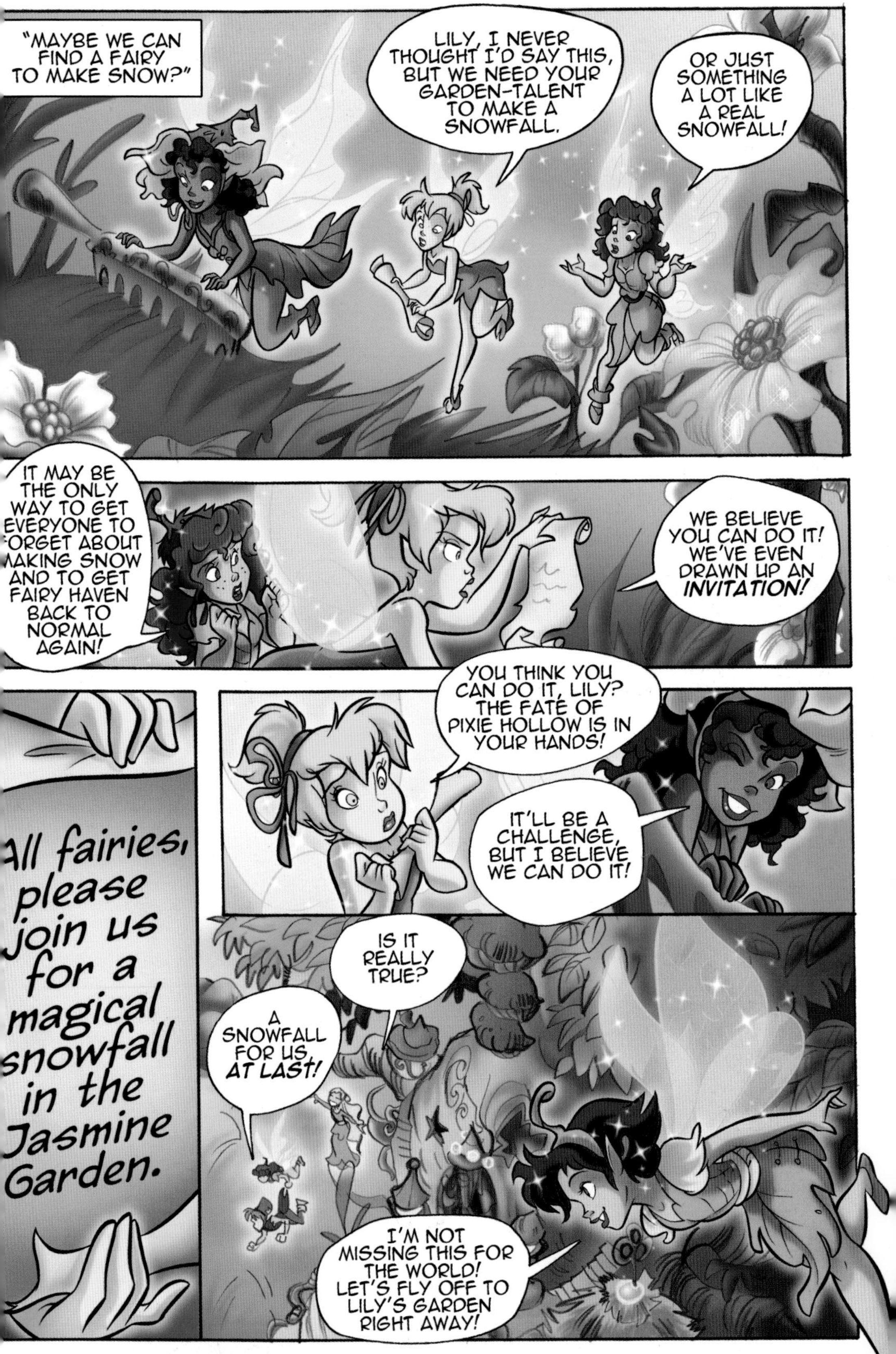
"MAYBE WE CAN FIND A FAIRY TO MAKE SNOW?"
LILY, I NEVER THOUGHT I'D SAY THIS, BUT WE NEED YOUR GARDEN-TALENT TO MAKE A SNOWFALL.
OR JUST SOMETHING A LOT LIKE A REAL SNOWFALL!
IT MAY BE THE ONLY WAY TO GET EVERYONE TO FORGET ABOUT MAKING SNOW AND TO GET FAIRY HAVEN BACK TO NORMAL AGAIN!
WE BELIEVE YOU CAN DO IT! WE'VE EVEN DRAWN UP AN *INVITATION!*
All fairies, please join us for a magical snowfall in the Jasmine Garden.
YOU THINK YOU CAN DO IT, LILY? THE FATE OF PIXIE HOLLOW IS IN YOUR HANDS!
IT'LL BE A CHALLENGE, BUT I BELIEVE WE CAN DO IT!
IS IT REALLY TRUE?
A SNOWFALL FOR US, *AT LAST!*
I'M NOT MISSING THIS FOR THE WORLD! LET'S FLY OFF TO LILY'S GARDEN RIGHT AWAY!

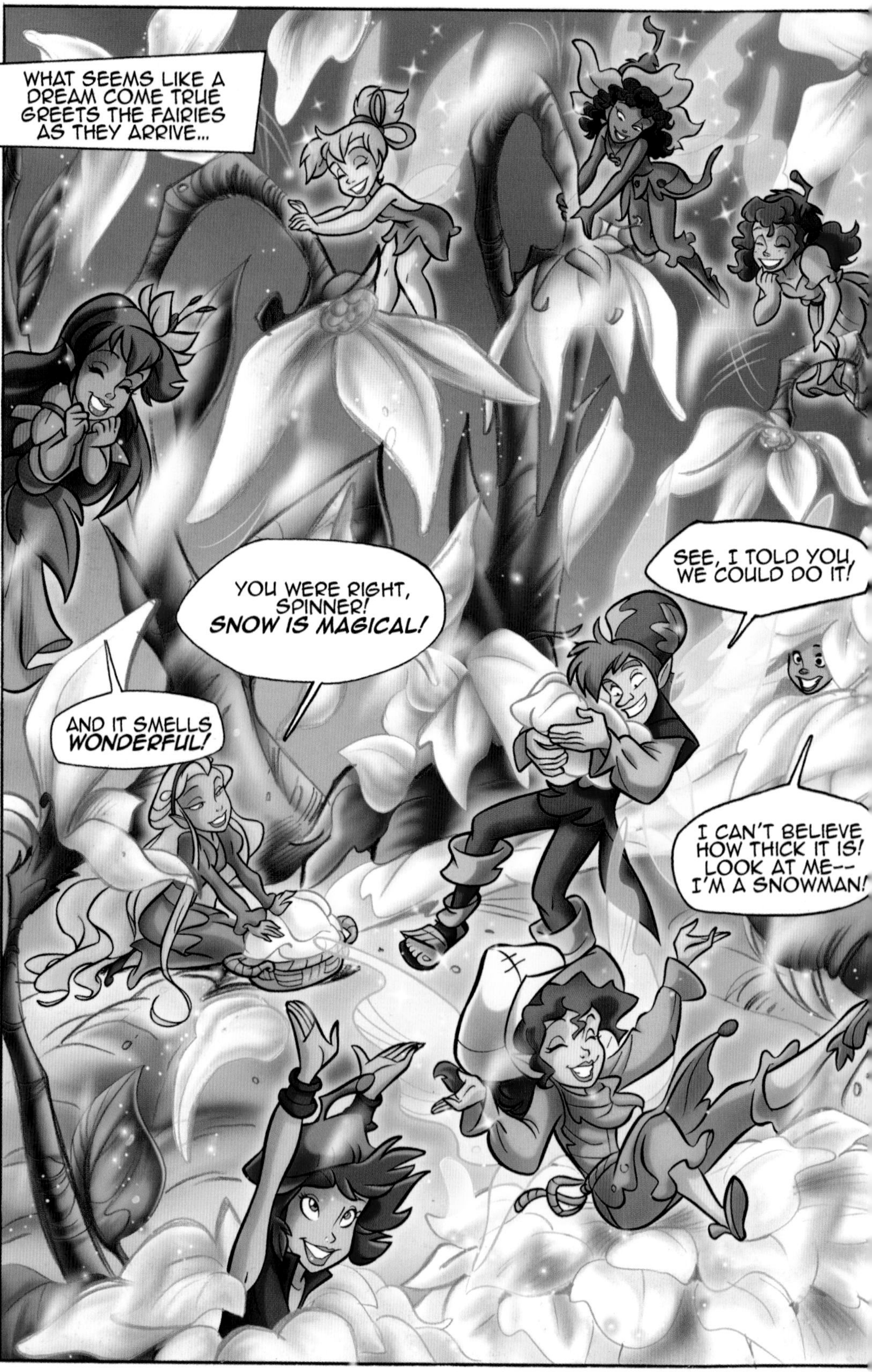
WHAT SEEMS LIKE A DREAM COME TRUE GREETS THE FAIRIES AS THEY ARRIVE...
YOU WERE RIGHT, SPINNER! SNOW IS MAGICAL!
SEE, I TOLD YOU, WE COULD DO IT!
AND IT SMELLS WONDERFUL!
I CAN'T BELIEVE HOW THICK IT IS! LOOK AT ME-- I'M A SNOWMAN!

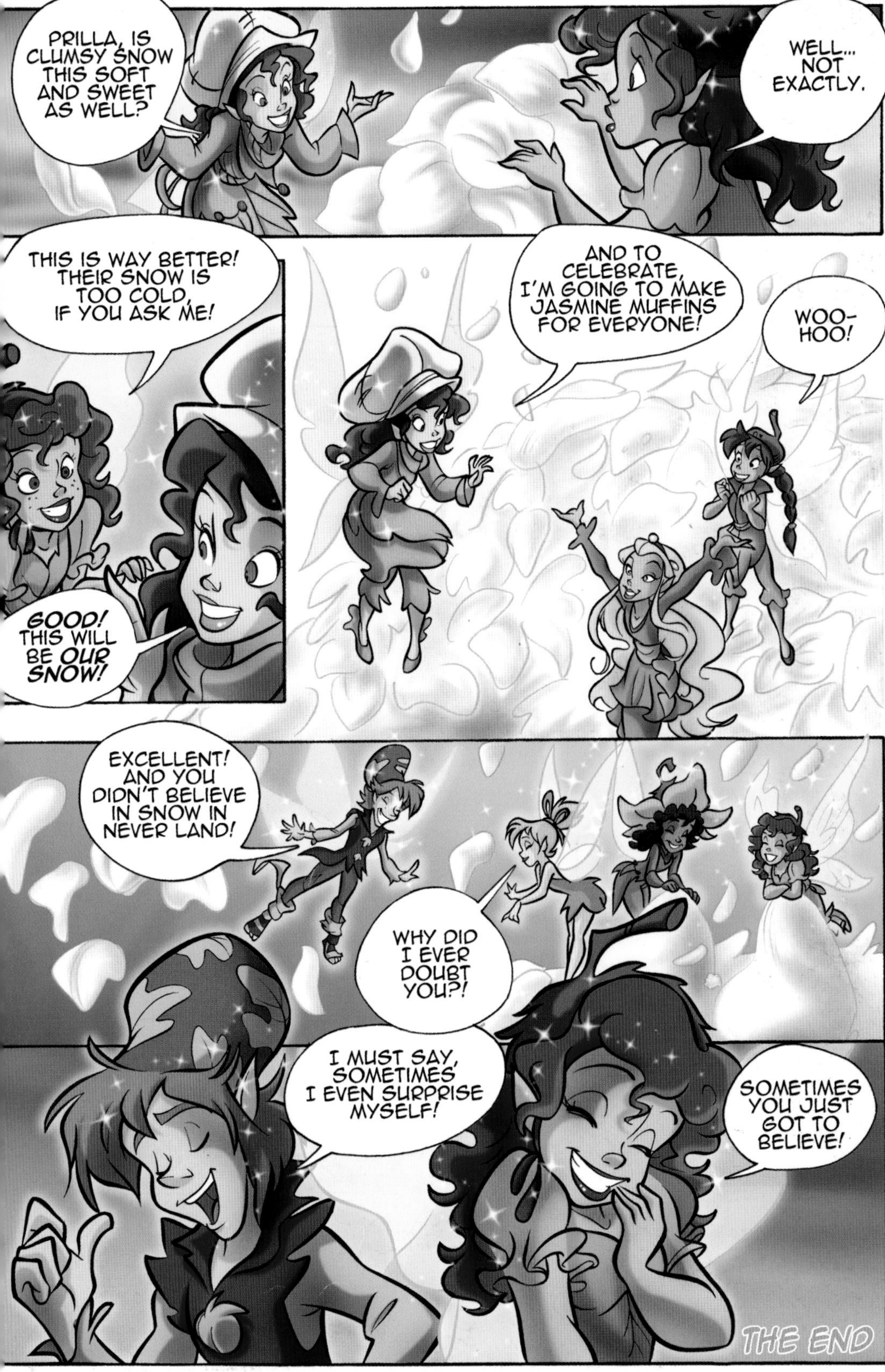
PRILLA, IS CLUMSY SNOW THIS SOFT AND SWEET AS WELL?
WELL... NOT EXACTLY.
THIS IS WAY BETTER! THEIR SNOW IS TOO COLD, IF YOU ASK ME!
GOOD! THIS WILL BE OUR SNOW!
AND TO CELEBRATE, I'M GOING TO MAKE JASMINE MUFFINS FOR EVERYONE!
WOO-HOO!
EXCELLENT! AND YOU DIDN'T BELIEVE IN SNOW IN NEVER LAND!
WHY DID I EVER DOUBT YOU?!
I MUST SAY, SOMETIMES I EVEN SURPRISE MYSELF!
SOMETIMES YOU JUST GOT TO BELIEVE!
THE END

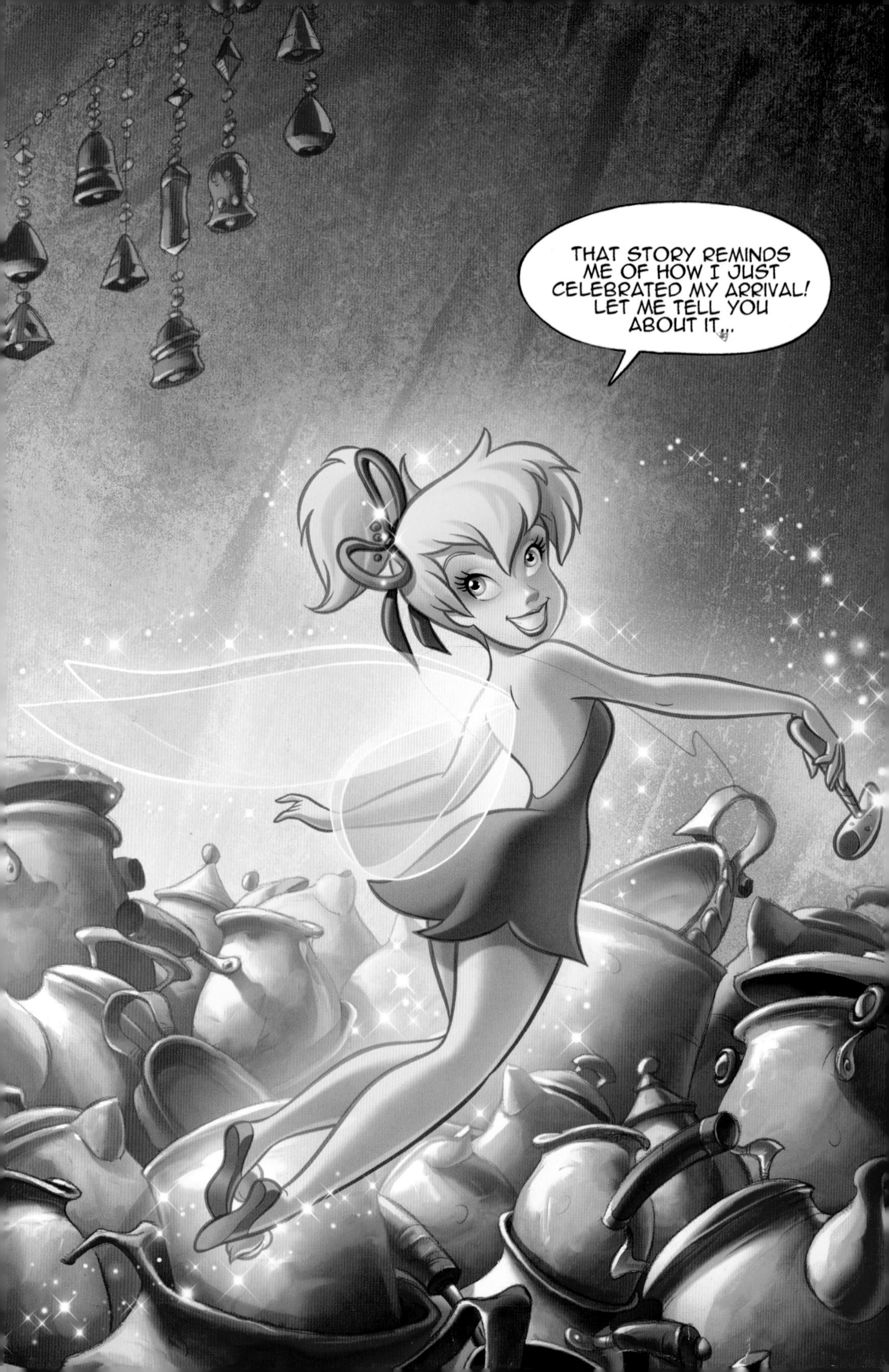
THAT STORY REMINDS ME OF HOW I JUST CELEBRATED MY ARRIVAL! LET ME TELL YOU ABOUT IT...

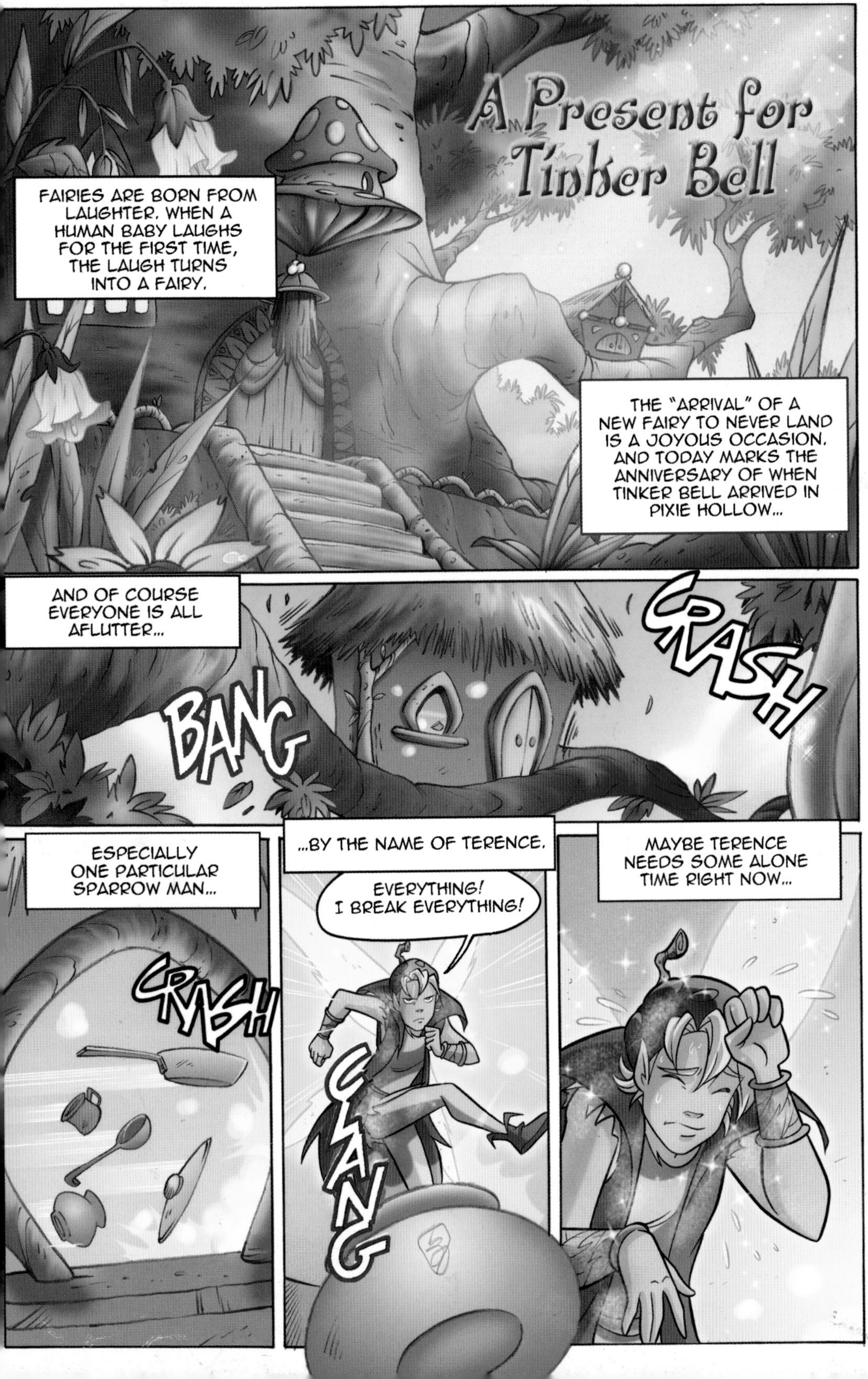
A Present for Tinker Bell
FAIRIES ARE BORN FROM LAUGHTER. WHEN A HUMAN BABY LAUGHS FOR THE FIRST TIME, THE LAUGH TURNS INTO A FAIRY.
THE "ARRIVAL" OF A NEW FAIRY TO NEVER LAND IS A JOYOUS OCCASION. AND TODAY MARKS THE ANNIVERSARY OF WHEN TINKER BELL ARRIVED IN PIXIE HOLLOW...
AND OF COURSE EVERYONE IS ALL AFLUTTER...
CRASH
BANG
ESPECIALLY ONE PARTICULAR SPARROW MAN...
CRASH
...BY THE NAME OF TERENCE.
EVERYTHING! I BREAK EVERYTHING!
CLANG
MAYBE TERENCE NEEDS SOME ALONE TIME RIGHT NOW...

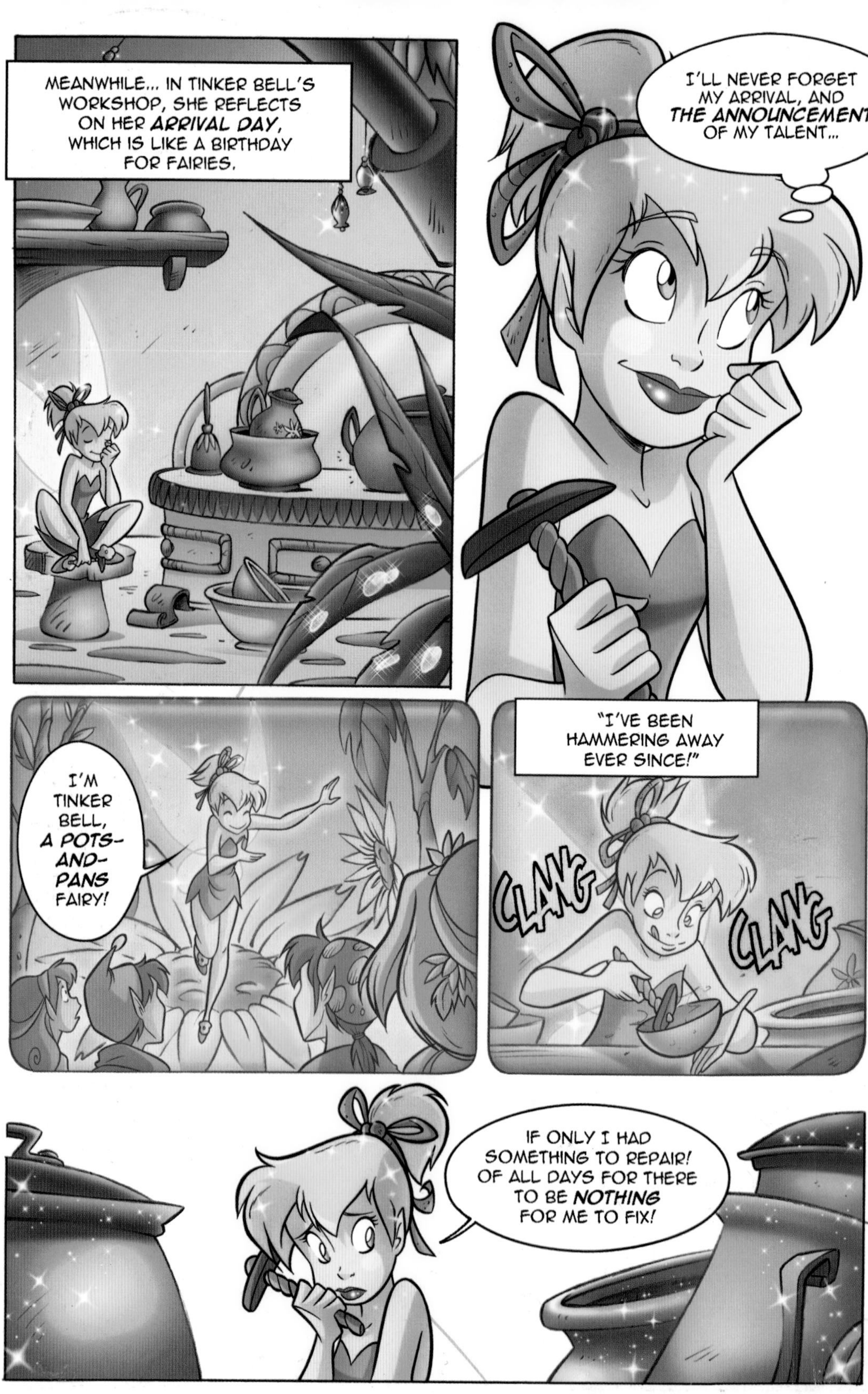
MEANWHILE... IN TINKER BELL'S WORKSHOP, SHE REFLECTS ON HER ARRIVAL DAY, WHICH IS LIKE A BIRTHDAY FOR FAIRIES.
I'LL NEVER FORGET MY ARRIVAL, AND THE ANNOUNCEMENT OF MY TALENT...
I'M TINKER BELL, A POTS-AND-PANS FAIRY!
"I'VE BEEN HAMMERING AWAY EVER SINCE!"
CLANG
CLANG
IF ONLY I HAD SOMETHING TO REPAIR! OF ALL DAYS FOR THERE TO BE NOTHING FOR ME TO FIX!

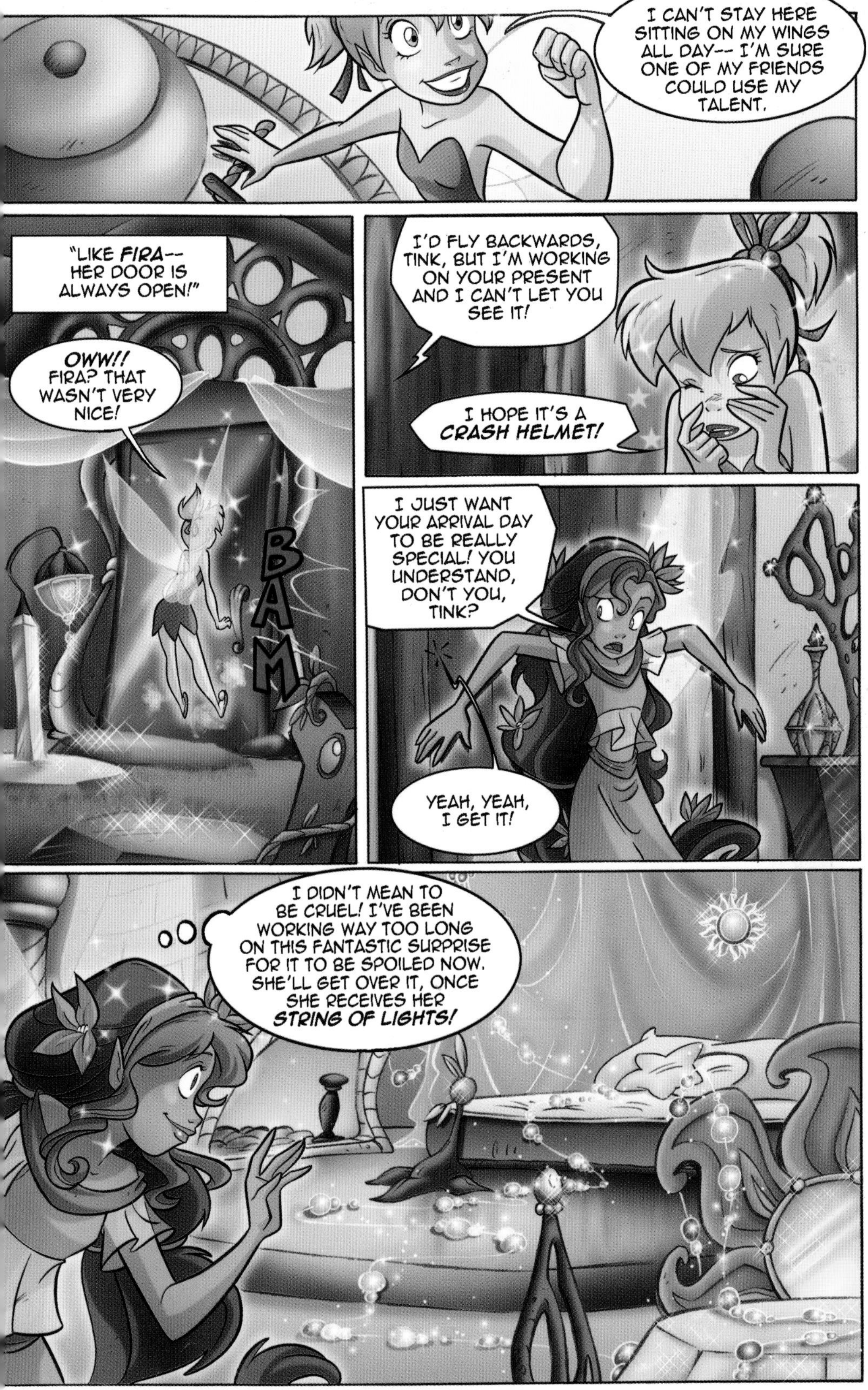
I CAN'T STAY HERE SITTING ON MY WINGS ALL DAY-- I'M SURE ONE OF MY FRIENDS COULD USE MY TALENT.
"LIKE FIRA-- HER DOOR IS ALWAYS OPEN!"
OWW!! FIRA? THAT WASN'T VERY NICE!
BAM
I'D FLY BACKWARDS, TINK, BUT I'M WORKING ON YOUR PRESENT AND I CAN'T LET YOU SEE IT!
I HOPE IT'S A CRASH HELMET!
I JUST WANT YOUR ARRIVAL DAY TO BE REALLY SPECIAL! YOU UNDERSTAND, DON'T YOU, TINK?
YEAH, YEAH, I GET IT!
I DIDN'T MEAN TO BE CRUEL! I'VE BEEN WORKING WAY TOO LONG ON THIS FANTASTIC SURPRISE FOR IT TO BE SPOILED NOW. SHE'LL GET OVER IT, ONCE SHE RECEIVES HER STRING OF LIGHTS!

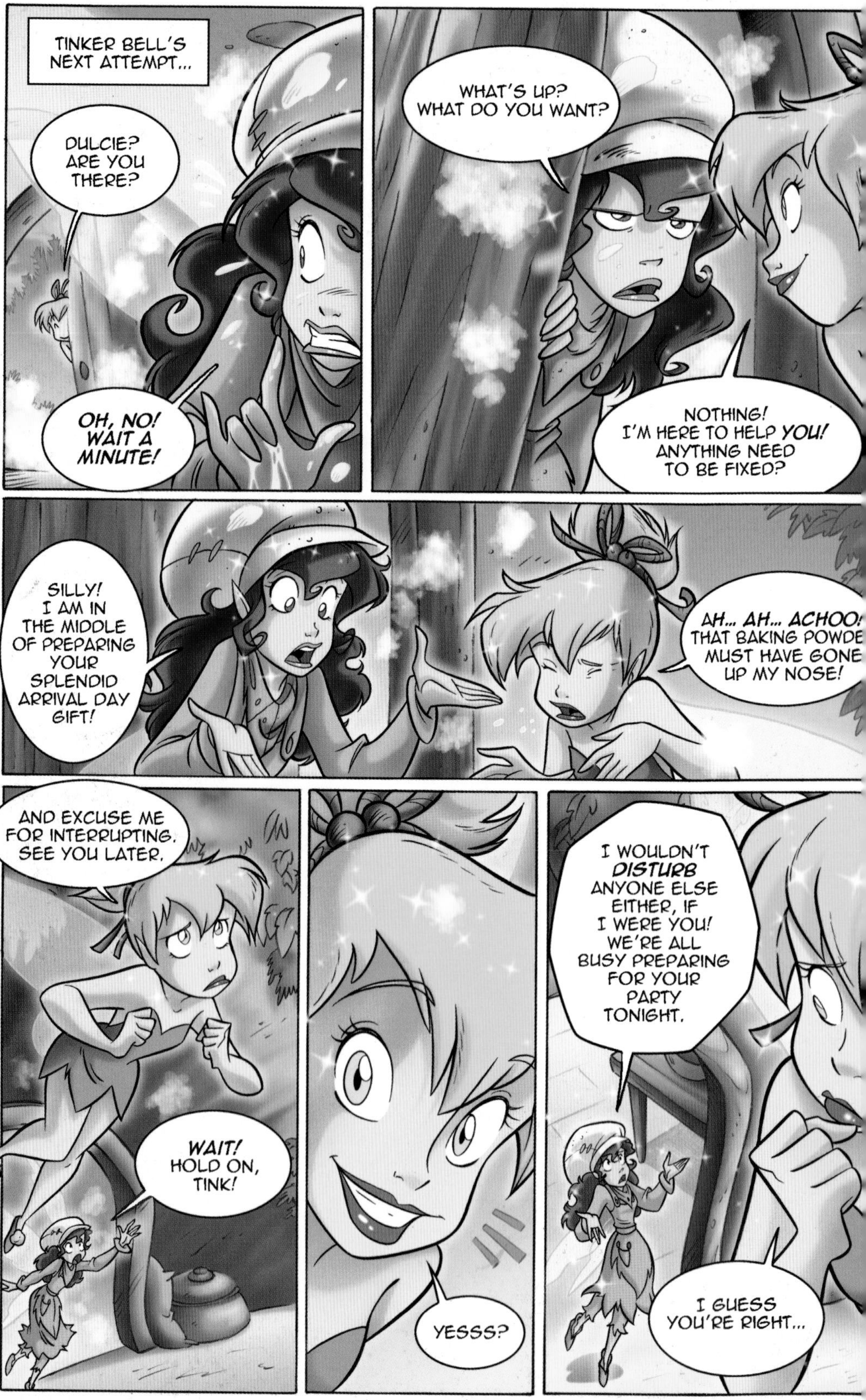
TINKER BELL'S NEXT ATTEMPT...
DULCIE? ARE YOU THERE?
OH, NO! WAIT A MINUTE!
WHAT'S UP? WHAT DO YOU WANT?
NOTHING! I'M HERE TO HELP YOU! ANYTHING NEED TO BE FIXED?
SILLY! I AM IN THE MIDDLE OF PREPARING YOUR SPLENDID ARRIVAL DAY GIFT!
AH... AH... ACHOO! THAT BAKING POWDE MUST HAVE GONE UP MY NOSE!
AND EXCUSE ME FOR INTERRUPTING. SEE YOU LATER.
WAIT! HOLD ON, TINK!
YESSS?
I WOULDN'T DISTURB ANYONE ELSE EITHER, IF I WERE YOU! WE'RE ALL BUSY PREPARING FOR YOUR PARTY TONIGHT.
I GUESS YOU'RE RIGHT...

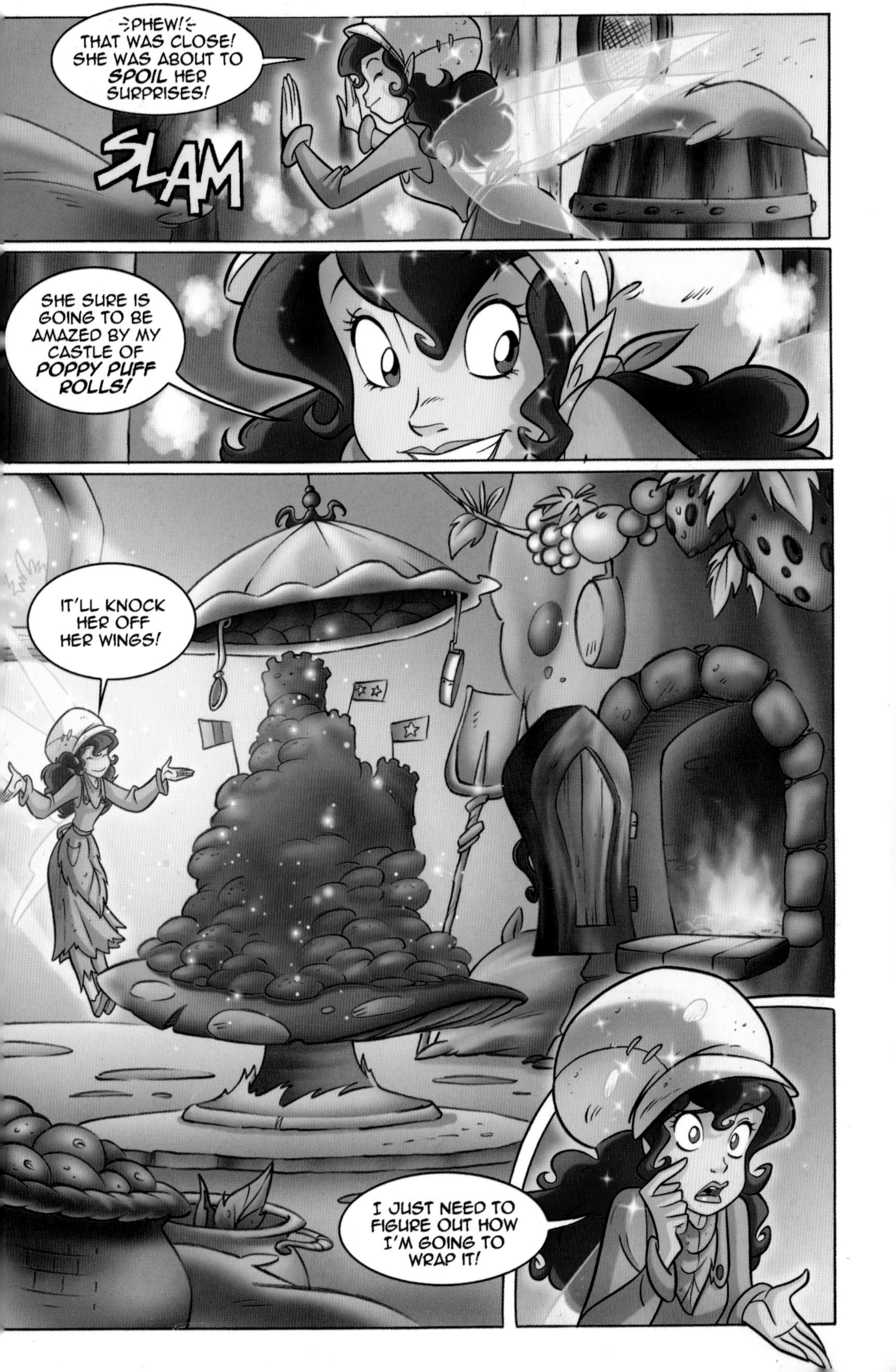
PHEW! THAT WAS CLOSE! SHE WAS ABOUT TO SPOIL HER SURPRISES!
SLAM
SHE SURE IS GOING TO BE AMAZED BY MY CASTLE OF POPPY PUFF ROLLS!
IT'LL KNOCK HER OFF HER WINGS!
I JUST NEED TO FIGURE OUT HOW I'M GOING TO WRAP IT!

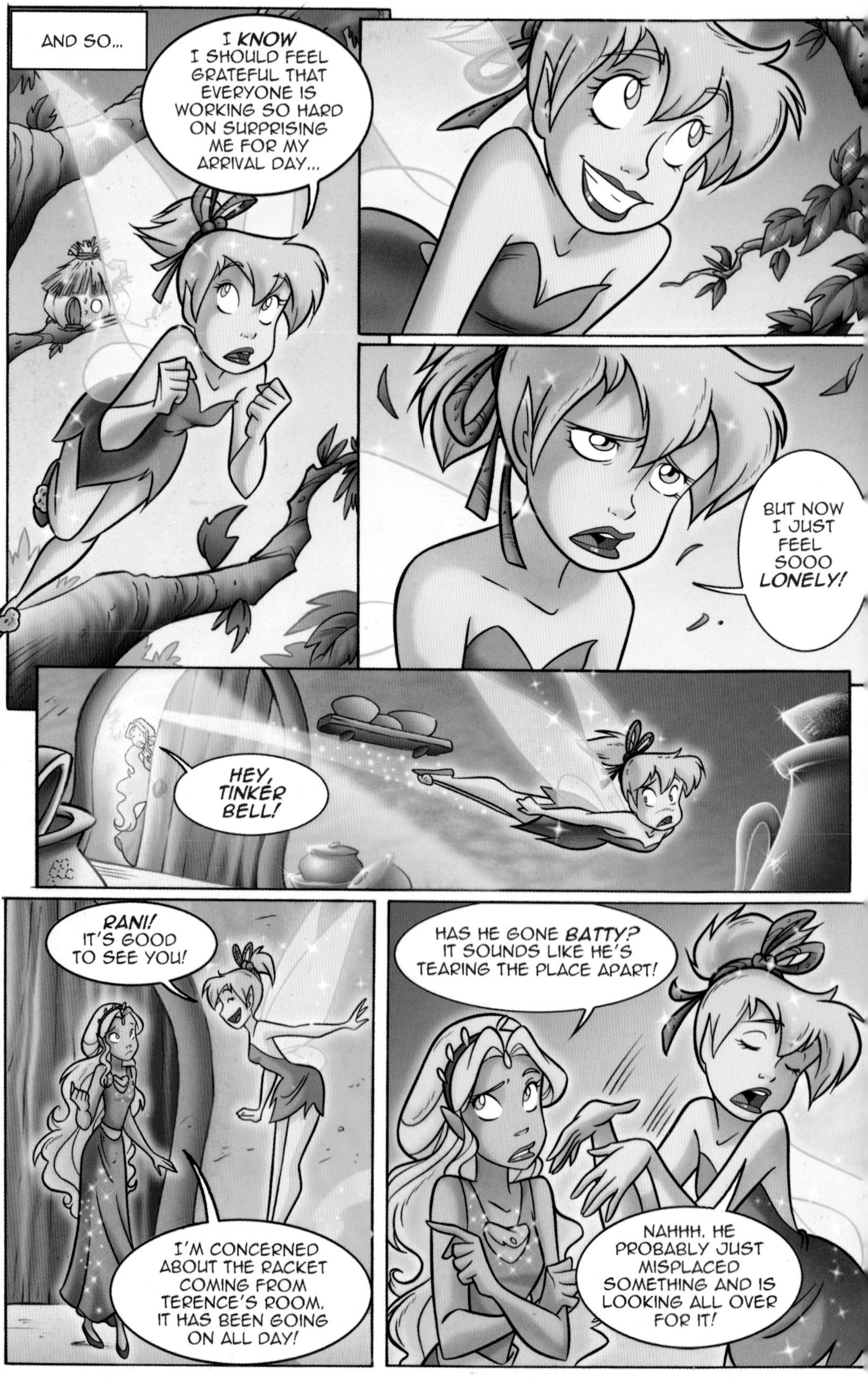
AND SO...
I KNOW I SHOULD FEEL GRATEFUL THAT EVERYONE IS WORKING SO HARD ON SURPRISING ME FOR MY ARRIVAL DAY...
BUT NOW I JUST FEEL SOOO LONELY!
HEY, TINKER BELL!
RANI! IT'S GOOD TO SEE YOU!
I'M CONCERNED ABOUT THE RACKET COMING FROM TERENCE'S ROOM. IT HAS BEEN GOING ON ALL DAY!
HAS HE GONE BATTY? IT SOUNDS LIKE HE'S TEARING THE PLACE APART!
NAHHH. HE PROBABLY JUST MISPLACED SOMETHING AND IS LOOKING ALL OVER FOR IT!

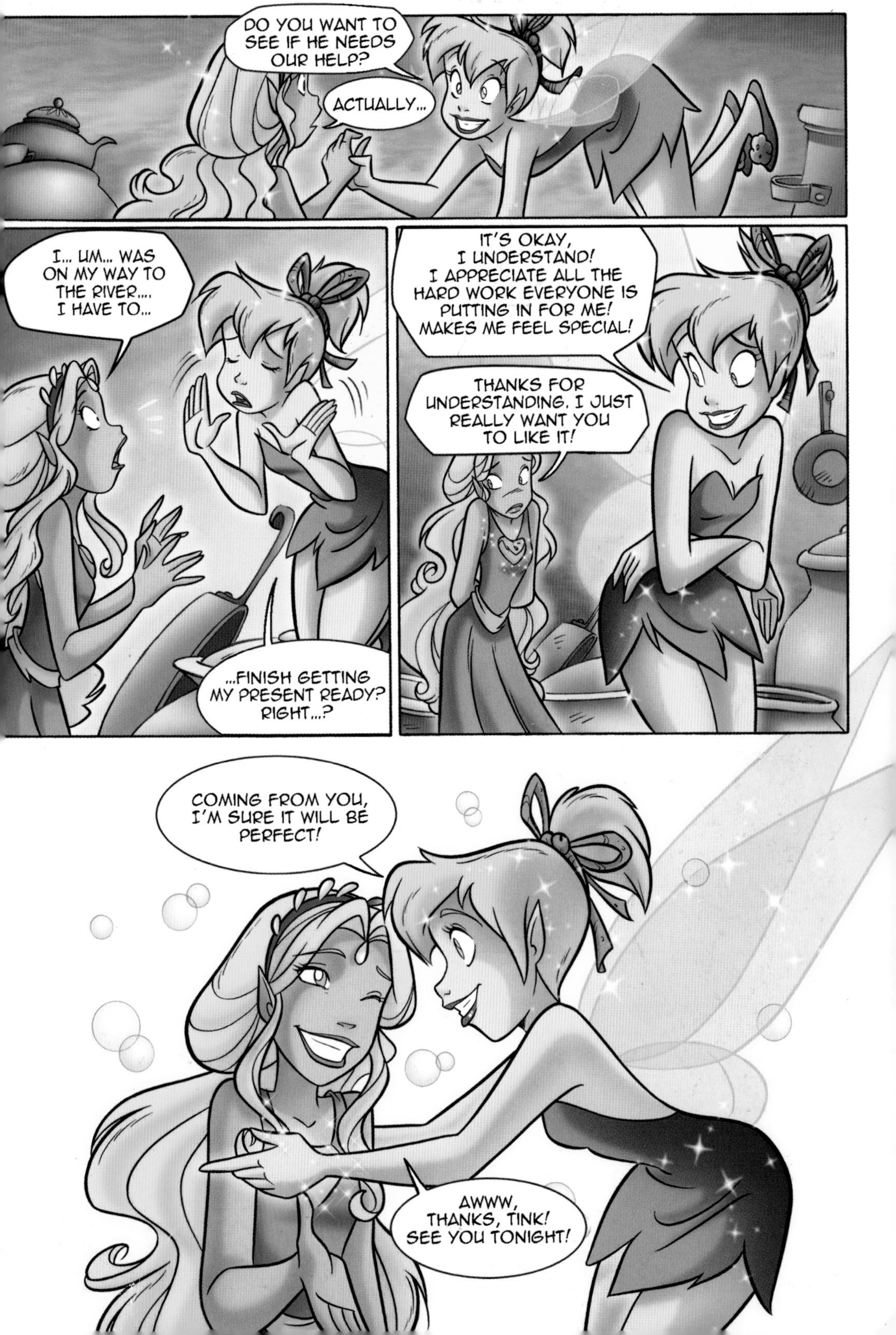
DO YOU WANT TO SEE IF HE NEEDS OUR HELP?
ACTUALLY...
I... UM... WAS ON MY WAY TO THE RIVER.... I HAVE TO...
...FINISH GETTING MY PRESENT READY? RIGHT...?
IT'S OKAY, I UNDERSTAND! I APPRECIATE ALL THE HARD WORK EVERYONE IS PUTTING IN FOR ME! MAKES ME FEEL SPECIAL!
THANKS FOR UNDERSTANDING. I JUST REALLY WANT YOU TO LIKE IT!
COMING FROM YOU, I'M SURE IT WILL BE PERFECT!
AWWW, THANKS, TINK! SEE YOU TONIGHT!

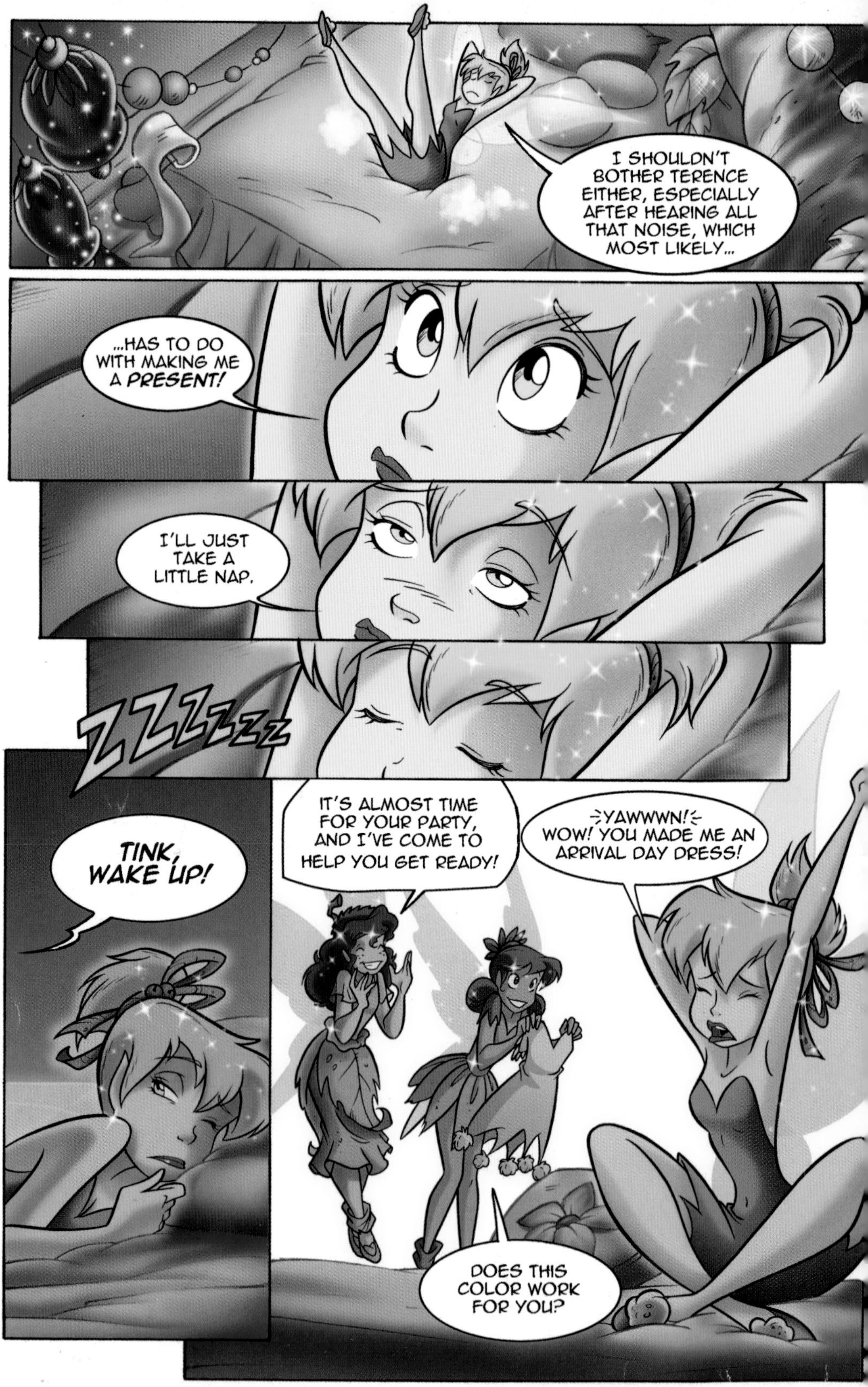
I SHOULDN'T BOTHER TERENCE EITHER, ESPECIALLY AFTER HEARING ALL THAT NOISE, WHICH MOST LIKELY...
...HAS TO DO WITH MAKING ME A *PRESENT*!
I'LL JUST TAKE A LITTLE NAP.
ZZZzzz
TINK, WAKE UP!
IT'S ALMOST TIME FOR YOUR PARTY, AND I'VE COME TO HELP YOU GET READY!
YAWWWN! WOW! YOU MADE ME AN ARRIVAL DAY DRESS!
DOES THIS COLOR WORK FOR YOU?

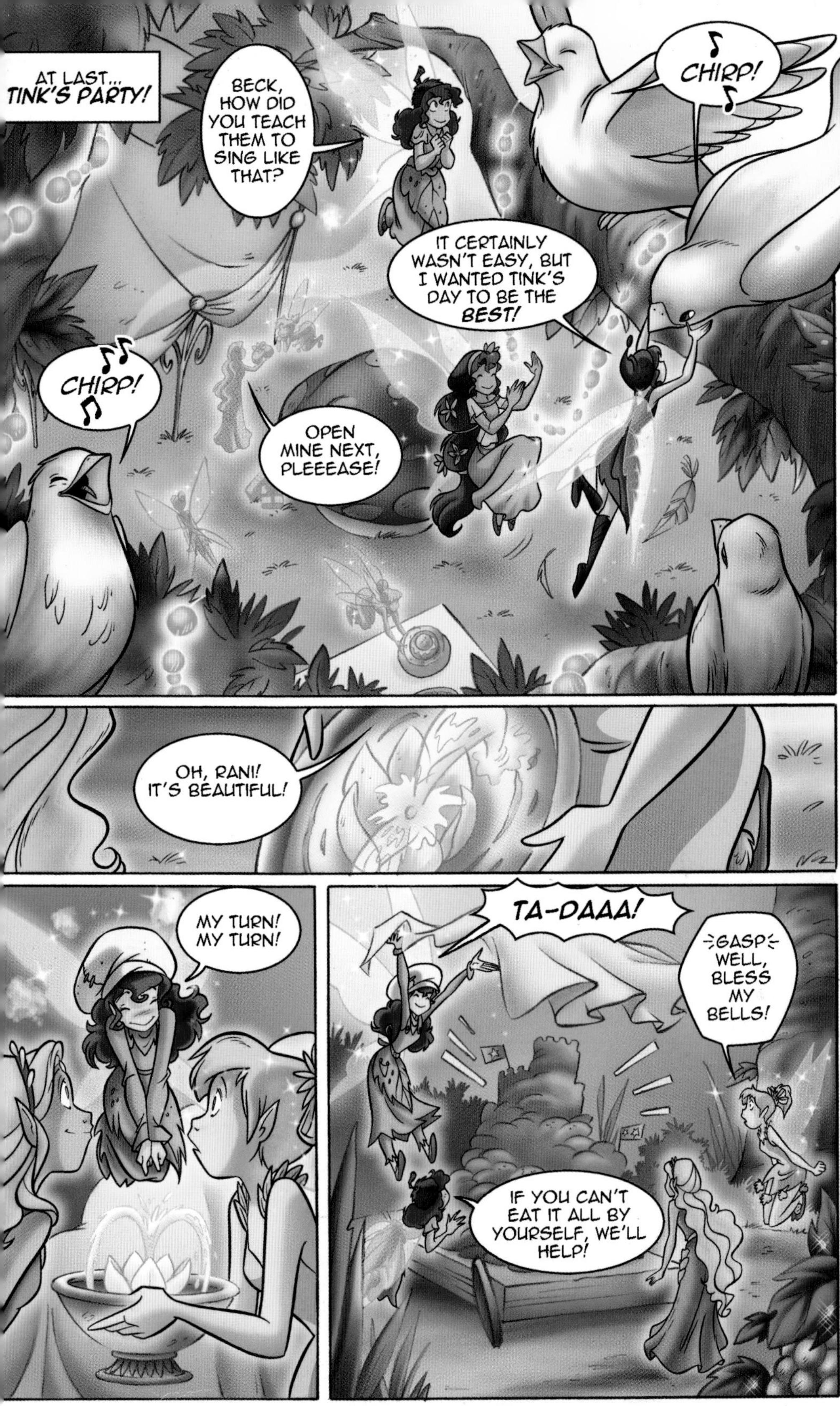
AT LAST... TINK'S PARTY!
BECK, HOW DID YOU TEACH THEM TO SING LIKE THAT?
CHIRP!
IT CERTAINLY WASN'T EASY, BUT I WANTED TINK'S DAY TO BE THE BEST!
CHIRP!
OPEN MINE NEXT, PLEEEASE!
OH, RANI! IT'S BEAUTIFUL!
MY TURN! MY TURN!
TA-DAAA!
GASP WELL, BLESS MY BELLS!
IF YOU CAN'T EAT IT ALL BY YOURSELF, WE'LL HELP!

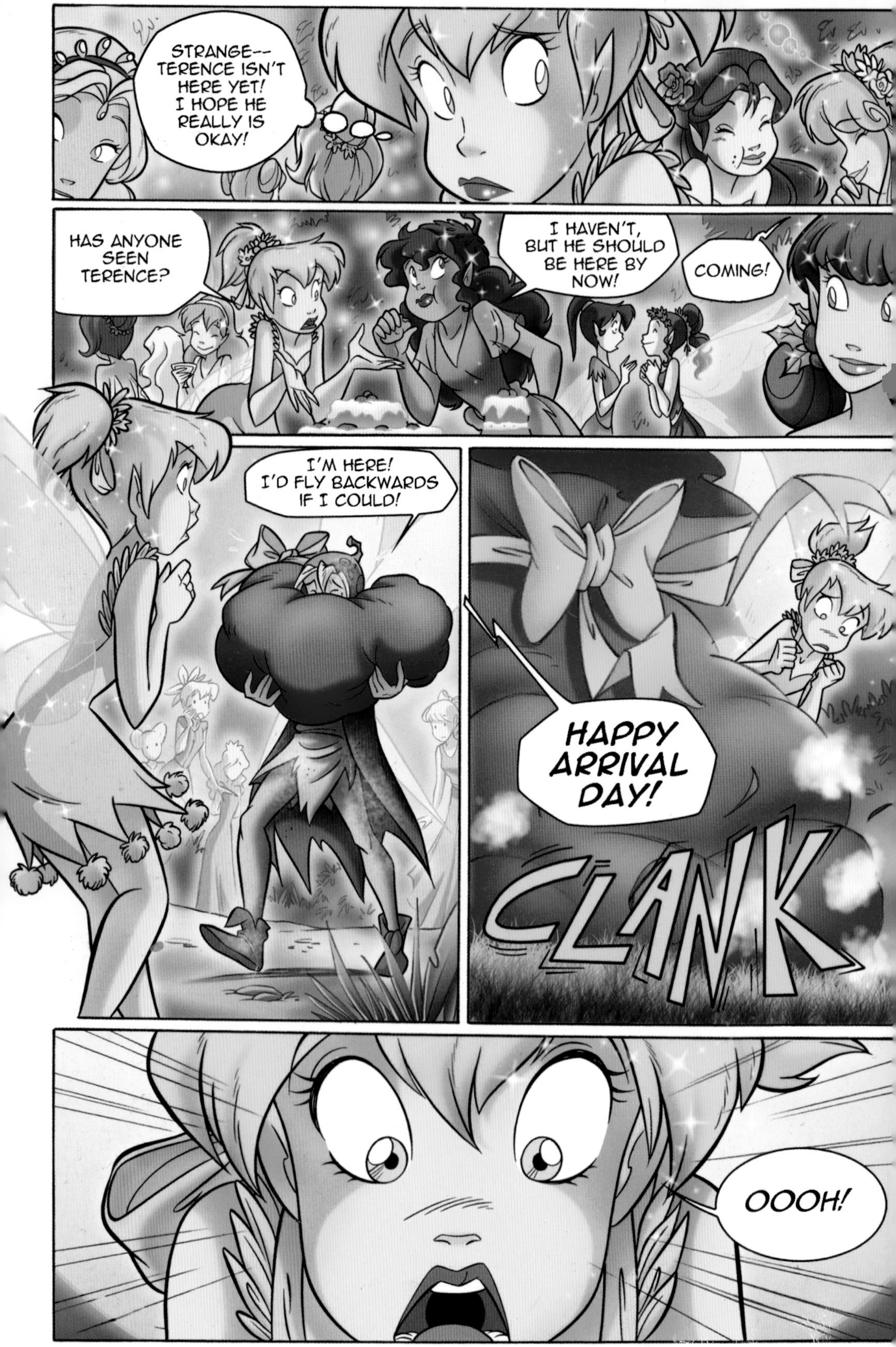
STRANGE-- TERENCE ISN'T HERE YET! I HOPE HE REALLY IS OKAY!
HAS ANYONE SEEN TERENCE?
I HAVEN'T, BUT HE SHOULD BE HERE BY NOW!
COMING!
I'M HERE! I'D FLY BACKWARDS IF I COULD!
HAPPY ARRIVAL DAY!
CLANK
OOOH!

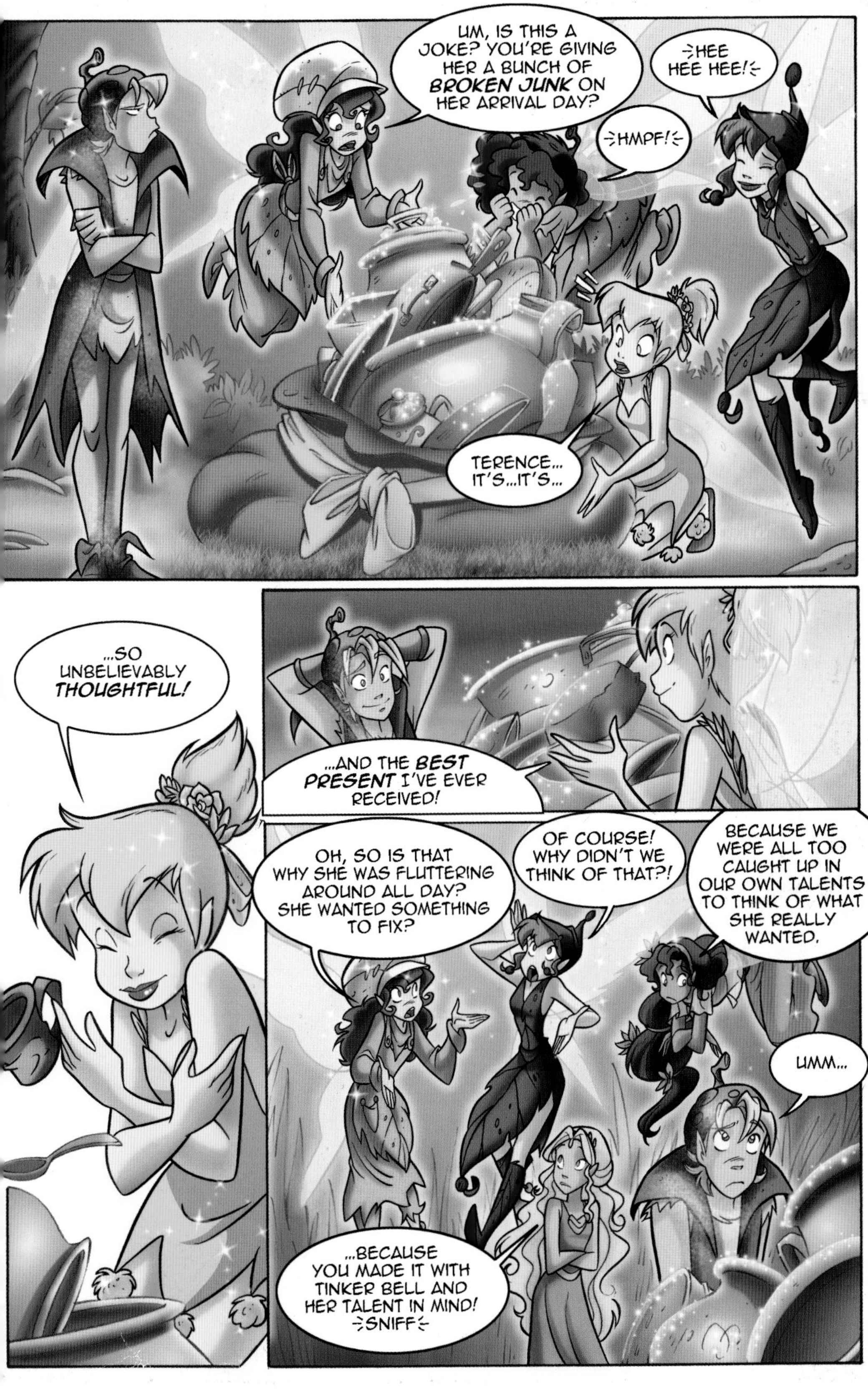
UM, IS THIS A JOKE? YOU'RE GIVING HER A BUNCH OF **BROKEN JUNK** ON HER ARRIVAL DAY?
HEE HEE HEE!
HMPF!
TERENCE... IT'S...IT'S...
...SO UNBELIEVABLY **THOUGHTFUL!**
...AND THE **BEST PRESENT** I'VE EVER RECEIVED!
OH, SO IS THAT WHY SHE WAS FLUTTERING AROUND ALL DAY? SHE WANTED SOMETHING TO FIX?
OF COURSE! WHY DIDN'T WE THINK OF THAT?!
BECAUSE WE WERE ALL TOO CAUGHT UP IN OUR OWN TALENTS TO THINK OF WHAT SHE REALLY WANTED.
UMM...
...BECAUSE YOU MADE IT WITH TINKER BELL AND HER TALENT IN MIND!
SNIFF

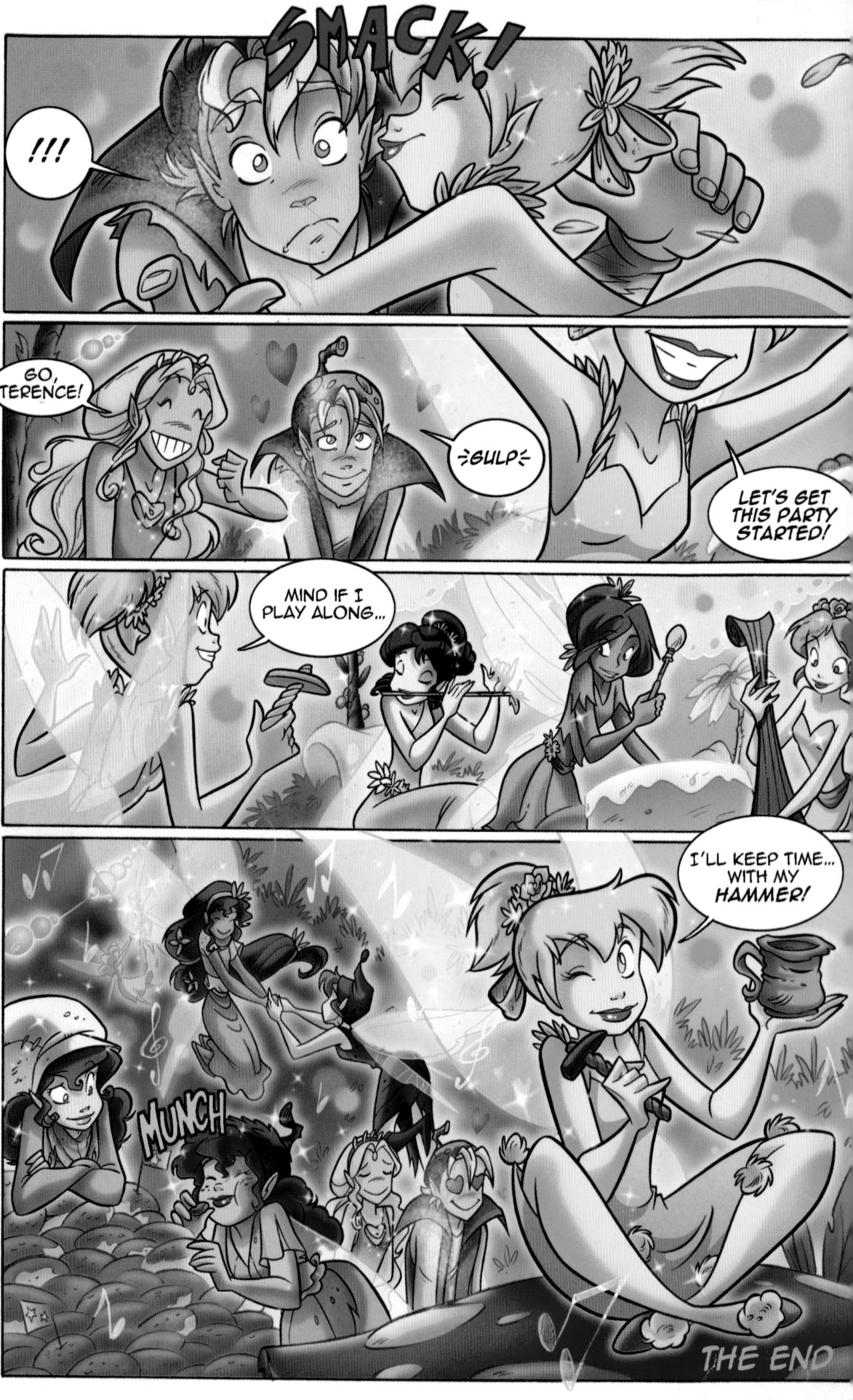
SMACK!
!!!
GO, TERENCE!
GULP
LET'S GET THIS PARTY STARTED!
MIND IF I PLAY ALONG...
I'LL KEEP TIME... WITH MY HAMMER!
MUNCH
THE END

WATCH OUT FOR

PAPERCUTZ™

Welcome to the sixth scintillating DISNEY FAIRIES graphic novel from Papercutz. I'm Jim Salicrup, your seemingly perpetually-pooped Papercutz Editor-in-Chief, and Pixie Hollow tour guide. Even though this is indeed our sixth DISNEY FAIRIES graphic novel, it's only our second at our new size. Or our third if you count the TINKER BELL AND THE GREAT FAIRY RESCUE graphic novel. While we're as thrilled as can be with how spectacular the great artwork by Marina Baggio, Caterina Giorgetti, Cristina Giorgilli, Elisabetta Melaranci, Manuela Razzi, Emilio Urbano, Roberta Zanotta, and others, looks on our bigger pages, it's really your opinion that matters most! Yes, you! If we're not doing absolutely everything we possibly can to keep you, and your fellow fairy-fans happy, then we want you to tell us! You can e-mail me directly at salicrup@papercutz.com and let me know what you think. Or you can send me an old-fashioned hand-written letter—just send it too Jim Salicrup, Papercutz, Ste. 1308, New York, NY 10005. Or you can even visit us at www.papercutz.com. Of course, you can also write us to tell us you love DISNEY FAIRIES too!

Speaking of the TINKER BELL AND THE GREAT FAIRY RESCUE graphic novel, the full-color comics adaptation of the third thrill-packed Tinker Bell DVD, I should warn you that it's becoming harder and harder to find! If you haven't picked up your copy yet, I suggest that you don't wait too much longer. While most enlightened bookstore and comicbookstore owners make sure to keep plenty of copies available of the DISNEY FAIRIES graphic novels, a few may think that TINKER BELL AND THE GREAT FAIRY RESCUE is nothing more than a quickie tie-in to the DVD, and not the beautifully designed graphic novel that's just as appealing today as it was when first published. Remember, if your friendly neighbourhood bookstore or comicbook store is out of stock, they can still order you a copy—or you can always order from your favorite online bookseller. And furthermore, what do you think about Papercutz publishing graphic novel adaptations of the earlier Tinker Bell DVDS? Write and let us know!

Now, before we run out of room, we have a couple of really exciting announcements: First, are you aware that there is a beautiful *Tinker Bell* magazine published eight times a year? It's a magazine filled with fairy fun, pixie puzzles, crafts, posters, activities, and stories! Check out the special offer on page 64 and see how you can save up to 50% off the cover price by subscribing and how you can get a free issue!

And finally, in answer to your countless requests, we're happy to announce that there's a special guest-star scheduled to appear in the very next DISNEY FAIRIES graphic novel! It's someone you've been demanding to see since our very first DISNEY FAIRIES graphic novel. Can you guess who it is? We'll just give you one big clue—our surprise guest is a special someone from Tinker Bell's past—and it's NOT Captain Hook!

So, until we meet again, don't forget to keep believing in "Faith, Trust, and Pixie Dust"!

Thanks,

Jim

Special Preview of DISNEY FAIRIES Graphic Novel #7 "Tinker Bell the Perfect Fairy"

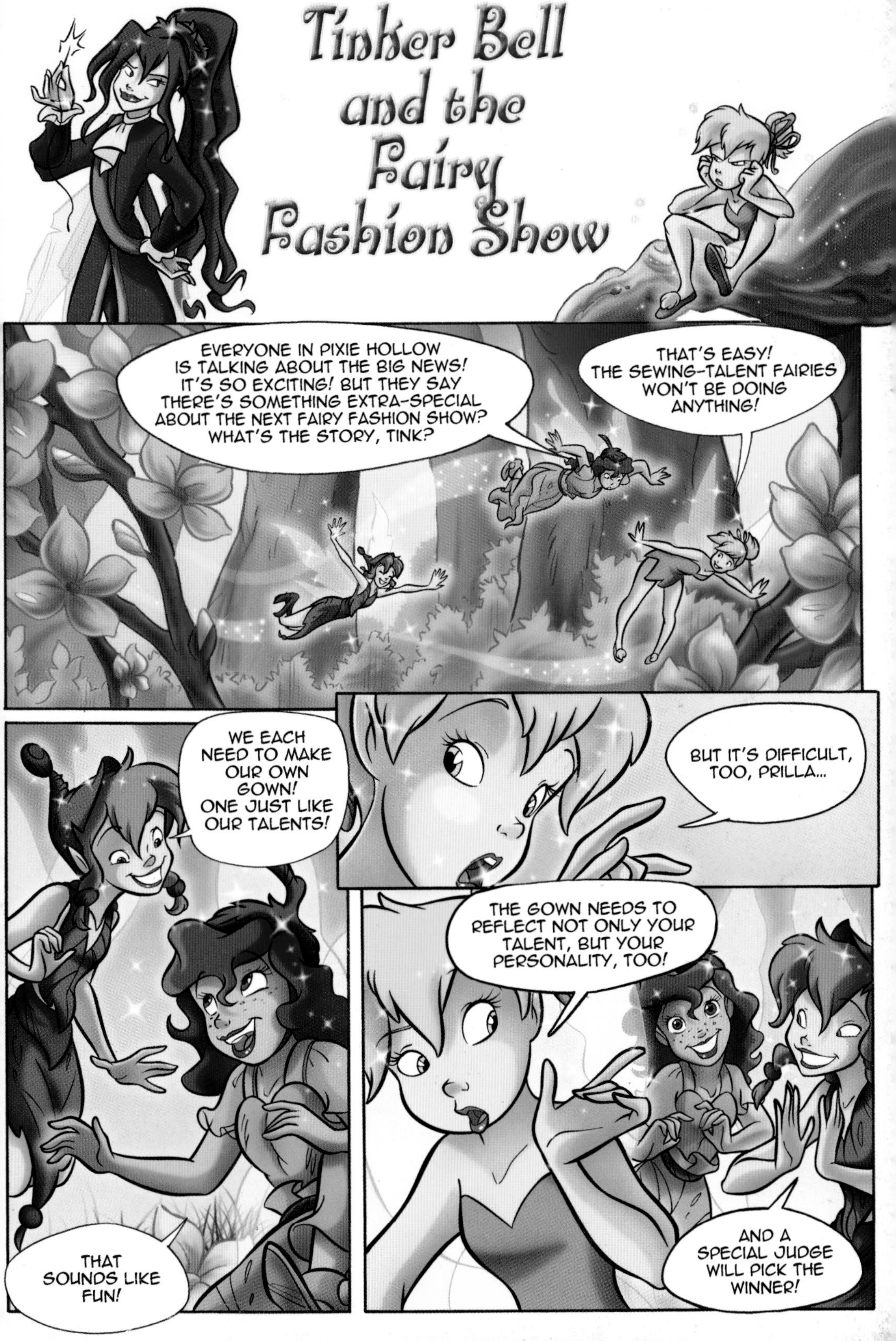
Tinker Bell and the Fairy Fashion Show
EVERYONE IN PIXIE HOLLOW IS TALKING ABOUT THE BIG NEWS! IT'S SO EXCITING! BUT THEY SAY THERE'S SOMETHING EXTRA-SPECIAL ABOUT THE NEXT FAIRY FASHION SHOW? WHAT'S THE STORY, TINK?
THAT'S EASY! THE SEWING-TALENT FAIRIES WON'T BE DOING ANYTHING!
WE EACH NEED TO MAKE OUR OWN GOWN! ONE JUST LIKE OUR TALENTS!
THAT SOUNDS LIKE FUN!
BUT IT'S DIFFICULT, TOO, PRILLA...
THE GOWN NEEDS TO REFLECT NOT ONLY YOUR TALENT, BUT YOUR PERSONALITY, TOO!
AND A SPECIAL JUDGE WILL PICK THE WINNER!

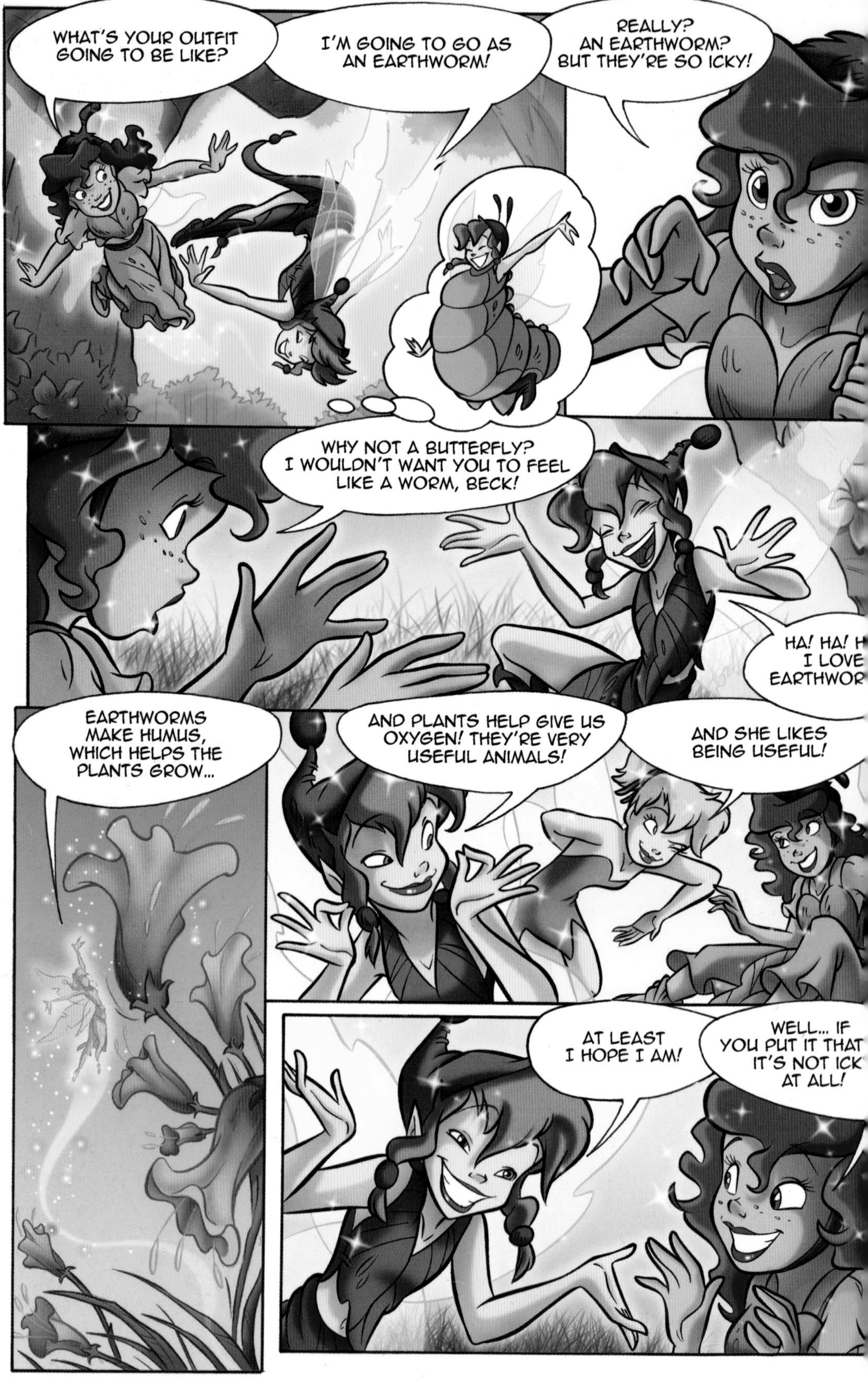
WHAT'S YOUR OUTFIT GOING TO BE LIKE?
I'M GOING TO GO AS AN EARTHWORM!
REALLY? AN EARTHWORM? BUT THEY'RE SO ICKY!
WHY NOT A BUTTERFLY? I WOULDN'T WANT YOU TO FEEL LIKE A WORM, BECK!
HA! HA! H
I LOVE
EARTHWOR
EARTHWORMS MAKE HUMUS, WHICH HELPS THE PLANTS GROW...
AND PLANTS HELP GIVE US OXYGEN! THEY'RE VERY USEFUL ANIMALS!
AND SHE LIKES BEING USEFUL!
AT LEAST I HOPE I AM!
WELL... IF YOU PUT IT THAT IT'S NOT ICK AT ALL!

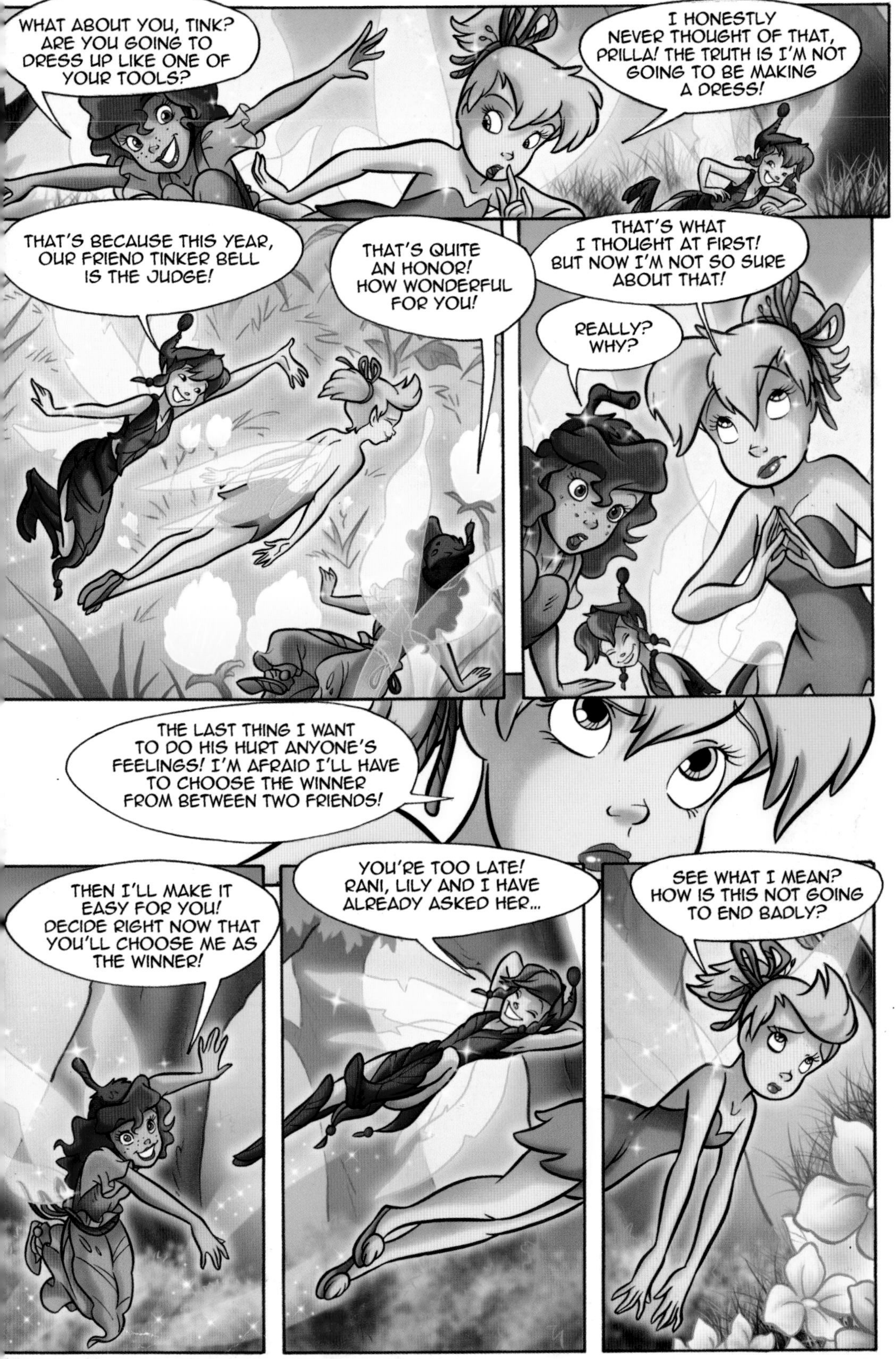
WHAT ABOUT YOU, TINK? ARE YOU GOING TO DRESS UP LIKE ONE OF YOUR TOOLS?
I HONESTLY NEVER THOUGHT OF THAT, PRILLA! THE TRUTH IS I'M NOT GOING TO BE MAKING A DRESS!
THAT'S BECAUSE THIS YEAR, OUR FRIEND TINKER BELL IS THE JUDGE!
THAT'S QUITE AN HONOR! HOW WONDERFUL FOR YOU!
THAT'S WHAT I THOUGHT AT FIRST! BUT NOW I'M NOT SO SURE ABOUT THAT!
REALLY? WHY?
THE LAST THING I WANT TO DO HIS HURT ANYONE'S FEELINGS! I'M AFRAID I'LL HAVE TO CHOOSE THE WINNER FROM BETWEEN TWO FRIENDS!
THEN I'LL MAKE IT EASY FOR YOU! DECIDE RIGHT NOW THAT YOU'LL CHOOSE ME AS THE WINNER!
YOU'RE TOO LATE! RANI, LILY AND I HAVE ALREADY ASKED HER...
SEE WHAT I MEAN? HOW IS THIS NOT GOING TO END BADLY?

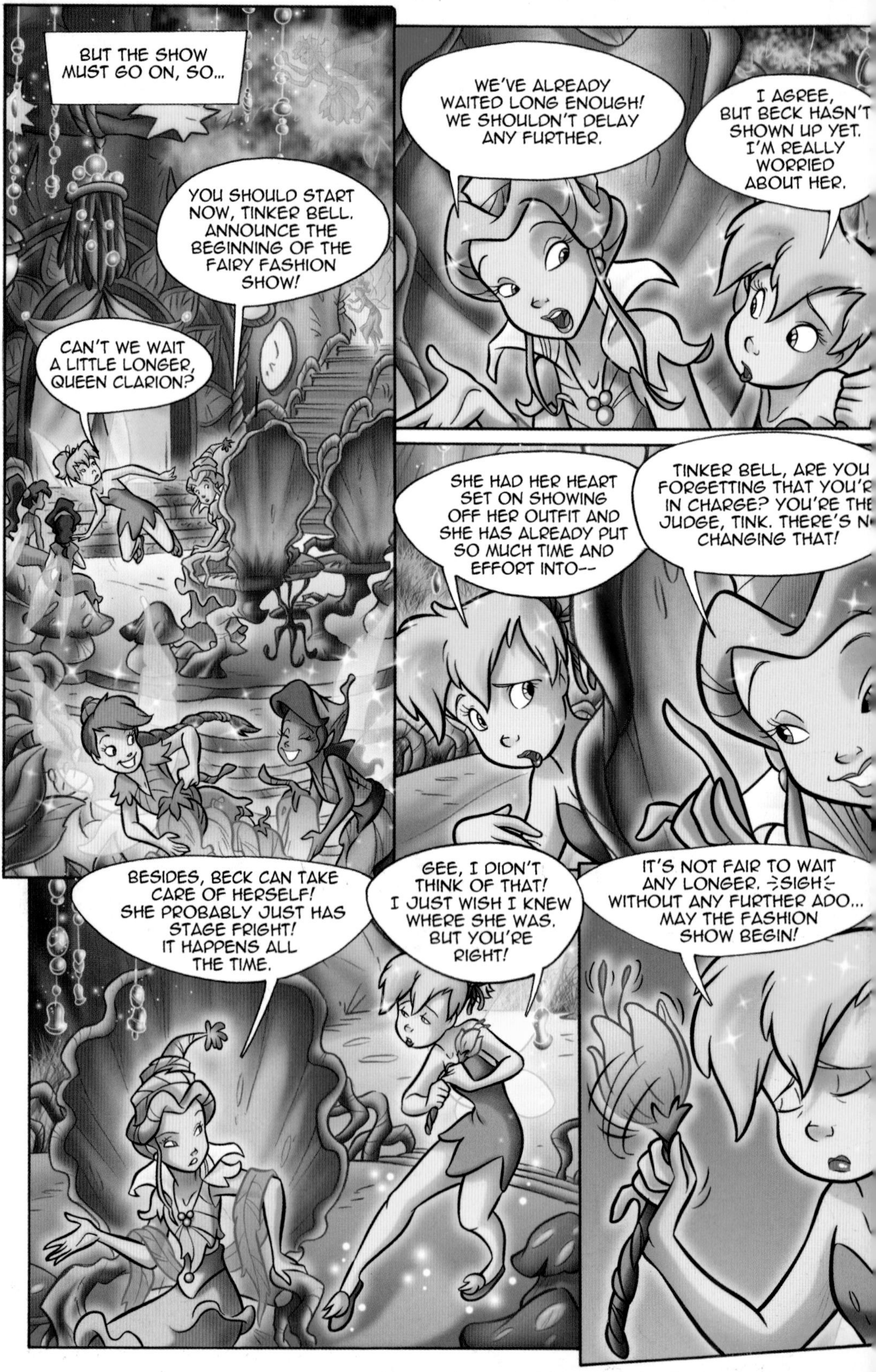
BUT THE SHOW MUST GO ON, SO...
YOU SHOULD START NOW, TINKER BELL. ANNOUNCE THE BEGINNING OF THE FAIRY FASHION SHOW!
CAN'T WE WAIT A LITTLE LONGER, QUEEN CLARION?
WE'VE ALREADY WAITED LONG ENOUGH! WE SHOULDN'T DELAY ANY FURTHER.
I AGREE, BUT BECK HASN'T SHOWN UP YET. I'M REALLY WORRIED ABOUT HER.
SHE HAD HER HEART SET ON SHOWING OFF HER OUTFIT AND SHE HAS ALREADY PUT SO MUCH TIME AND EFFORT INTO--
TINKER BELL, ARE YOU FORGETTING THAT YOU'R IN CHARGE? YOU'RE THE JUDGE, TINK. THERE'S N CHANGING THAT!
BESIDES, BECK CAN TAKE CARE OF HERSELF! SHE PROBABLY JUST HAS STAGE FRIGHT! IT HAPPENS ALL THE TIME.
GEE, I DIDN'T THINK OF THAT! I JUST WISH I KNEW WHERE SHE WAS. BUT YOU'RE RIGHT!
IT'S NOT FAIR TO WAIT ANY LONGER. ⇾SIGH⇽ WITHOUT ANY FURTHER ADO... MAY THE FASHION SHOW BEGIN!

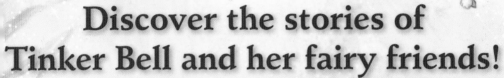

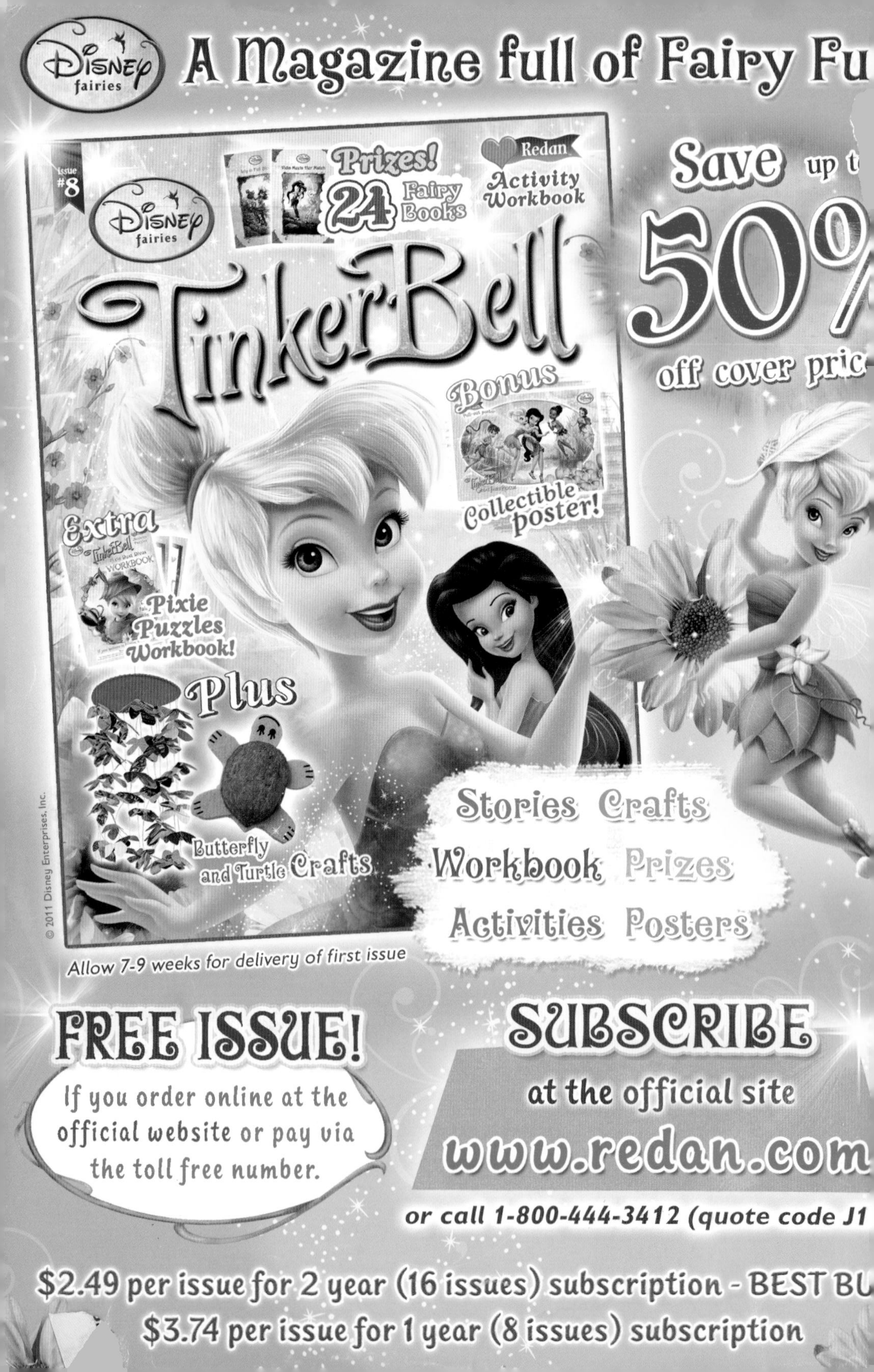
Disney fairies
A Magazine full of Fairy Fu
Save up t
50%
off cover pric
Issue #8
Disney fairies
Prizes! 24 Fairy Books
Redan
Activity Workbook
TinkerBell
Bonus
Collectible poster!
Extra
Pixie Puzzles Workbook!
Plus
Butterfly and Turtle Crafts
Stories Crafts
Workbook Prizes
Activities Posters
© 2011 Disney Enterprises, Inc.
Allow 7-9 weeks for delivery of first issue
FREE ISSUE!
If you order online at the official website or pay via the toll free number.
SUBSCRIBE
at the official site
www.redan.com
or call 1-800-444-3412 (quote code J1
$2.49 per issue for 2 year (16 issues) subscription - BEST BU
$3.74 per issue for 1 year (8 issues) subscription